*To Paula,
Thanks for [...]
I hope you enjoy it.*

Baz Black.

INK PRINCESS

Baz Black

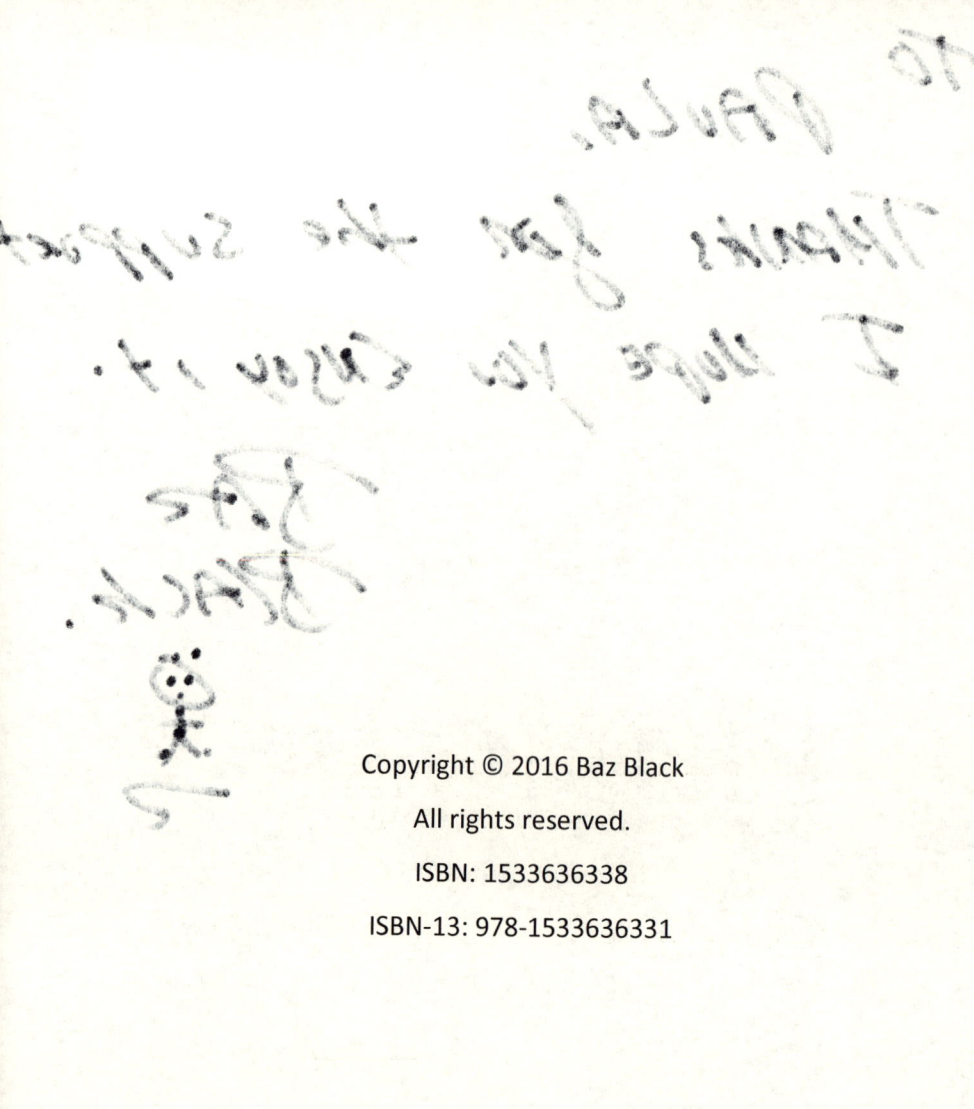

Copyright © 2016 Baz Black

All rights reserved.

ISBN: 1533636338

ISBN-13: 978-1533636331

ACKNOWLEDGMENTS

I would like to thank my family and friends for their support throughout the process of writing this book. A special thanks to my wife, Emma Ray, for drawing and designing the front cover, helping with layout and for putting up with my numerous mental breakdowns over the course of the year writing it.

Thank you to my editor, Krystal.
Thank you to WePrint.ie.
Author portrait photograph by Arthur Carron Photography.
Thank you to Dippy, Columbo, Summer and Bert inc.

And finally, thank you for buying, borrowing or stealing this book

CHAPTER ONE

Hi, my name is Megan Banks and last night I was a drunken, emotional mess. Please feel free to judge me accordingly. Fame does strange things to people, but I was already strange to begin with. I sit here in the sanctity of my local coffee shop, staring into my glorious cappuccino. It's frothy layer brings a little inward smile to my face. I am still way too hungover to force anything close to a real smile. Thoughts of dread and panic fill my body as I am reminded that today is the day. The day I have been dreading for months. Today I begin filming *The Megan Banks Story*. I cringe at the name. I am no stranger to cameras and TV crews at this stage, but I was always surrounded by my friends and family at the shop. This was me, front row and center, slice me open and spill my guts. As much as I try to stuff those guts back in, they are out for good for the world to see. My hands begin to sweat and I feel nauseous, the previous night's tequila slowly working its way back up my throat. I swallow hard to suppress the puke. I slow my breathing and get it together. That voice pops up inside my head again, *Come on you whiney little bitch, you wanted this. With great fame comes absolutely no responsibility. Ohh no, you have to go on television and talk about your life because people are actually interested in what you have to say?! Oh you poor thing!!! If I could slap you, I would...Pathetic.* The voice never used to be this aggressive before; I must be really pissing it off. My rambling thoughts are disrupted by a shrill shriek in my ear hole.

ACKNOWLEDGMENTS

I would like to thank my family and friends for their support throughout the process of writing this book. A special thanks to my wife, Emma Ray, for drawing and designing the front cover, helping with layout and for putting up with my numerous mental breakdowns over the course of the year writing it.

Thank you to my editor, Krystal.
Thank you to WePrint.ie.
Author portrait photograph by Arthur Carron Photography.
Thank you to Dippy, Columbo, Summer and Bert inc.

And finally, thank you for buying, borrowing or stealing this book

5 am and I am drunk again. I have become a cliché. My legs dangle precariously over the balcony ledge I am perched upon. The cool breeze of the summer's air is making my head spin. Fantasies of just letting go toy with my drunken mind. Who would notice? Who would even care? My subconscious mocks me as it always does, *Poor little Megan Banks, so melancholy in her infinite sadness. Do us all a favor and just fucking jump.* Another house, another party. Surrounded by hundreds of people but feel so alone. My feelings of self-loathing are momentarily distracted by the glimmer of the swimming pool below. The lights dance off the still water with elegance and beauty. I was always easily distracted. I have always thought my distractions have kept me sane, dropping in and out of my fantasy world to escape the pain of reality. Yes, I am quite aware of how self-involved I sound right now, but you don't know me – nobody knows me. Goose pimples shock my body back to the real world. How long have I been up here?

Neurotic and nauseous, I am cold and my body wants to sleep. Swinging my legs off my perched ledge, my feet make contact with solid ground once again. The drunk has started to leave my mind but clearly not my legs as they wobble and buckle beneath me. My mission is to find the comfort of a bed to rest my weary body. As I push open the large glass doors, the sharp noise of my heeled shoes on the wooden floor annoys me. I sit down and struggle with the straps to get them off. My body decides it is time to sleep. I lay my head on the cold floor, and immediately I am consumed with the sweet bliss of the sandman's kiss.

CHAPTER ONE

Hi, my name is Megan Banks and last night I was a drunken, emotional mess. Please feel free to judge me accordingly. Fame does strange things to people, but I was already strange to begin with. I sit here in the sanctity of my local coffee shop, staring into my glorious cappuccino. It's frothy layer brings a little inward smile to my face. I am still way too hungover to force anything close to a real smile. Thoughts of dread and panic fill my body as I am reminded that today is the day. The day I have been dreading for months. Today I begin filming *The Megan Banks Story*. I cringe at the name. I am no stranger to cameras and TV crews at this stage, but I was always surrounded by my friends and family at the shop. This was me, front row and center, slice me open and spill my guts. As much as I try to stuff those guts back in, they are out for good for the world to see. My hands begin to sweat and I feel nauseous, the previous night's tequila slowly working its way back up my throat. I swallow hard to suppress the puke. I slow my breathing and get it together. That voice pops up inside my head again, *Come on you whiney little bitch, you wanted this. With great fame comes absolutely no responsibility. Ohh no, you have to go on television and talk about your life because people are actually interested in what you have to say?! Oh you poor thing!!! If I could slap you, I would...Pathetic.* The voice never used to be this aggressive before; I must be really pissing it off. My rambling thoughts are disrupted by a shrill shriek in my ear hole.

"Oh my God, oh my God, I love you, like seriously I love you. You are like my inspiration! I'm going to be a tattoo artist just like you someday. Oh my God, I just had to come over. Can I touch you? Sorry, that's weird. I can't believe this is happening. I need to get a picture for my Facebook."

As my mind catches up with the young girl's rhetorical questions, I find myself politely posing for a picture and forcing that stubborn smile that wouldn't come earlier. "Take another one. Make sure you get it. Oh my God, this is actually happening." Her excitement had now captured the attention of the whole coffee shop and I feel a huge wave of embarrassment wash over me as I so often did.

"Aww, thank you, very nice to meet you," I say to her out of habit. With that, she dives in for a hug. I awkwardly retort with a side hug as a blocking technique. This was something I was forced to get used to when the TV show came along, but it has always been uncomfortable to me. I struggle with affection with loved ones, so to feign it with total strangers is foreign to me. Don't get me wrong, I always strive not to be rude and remain pleasant wherever possible, but I just don't like to be touched.

This was my cue to leave. As I pay for my coffee, I can feel everyone's eyes burn into my soul. I'm sure most of them were trying to figure out who the hell was this tattooed chick with lime green hair that had made the shrieking girl so excited. As I make my way towards the door, I keep my head down, partly out of embarrassment but mainly trying to keep that tequila down. I pull my hood tight as the rain beats down on my head. It actually feels quite refreshing. I have always loved the rain. I like how it keeps the streets quiet as people cower for shelter; I like how it makes me feel alive, the harder the better – come on world, show me what you've got!

As I reach my apartment block, I resemble a drowned rat. My black mascara runs from my eyes, making me look like a fifteen-year-old Goth (who is mad at their dad). I let out a little laugh as I catch a glimpse of my reflection on the elevator door. Oh Megan, if the cameras could only see you now.

I live on Fifth Avenue in an amazing penthouse apartment. This is my fourth apartment move since I have been here, but with its 24-hour security, it makes me feel safe, a feeling I have not had since my move to New York. I almost feel a wave of guilt getting to live here, but then I remind myself how hard I have worked for this and the guilt is subsided by joy. Manhattan is my new home, my second chance of life and it has embraced me with open arms.

I push open my apartment door and I am greeted by an old friend. His name is Jake. Jake is small, dark and handsome. He has been my rock through all of the madness. He's the only one who has sat with me while I shed my tears and has cheered me up whenever I was feeling down. I have never met anyone as kind and compassionate as him. He will spend hours unselfishly listening to my problems and will comfort me to the early hours of the morning. Truly, I would be lost without him. Jake is my cat. And right now he is pissed off with me.

"Who do you think you are, leaving me here alone all night? I was worried sick. That's why I haven't touched my food in the bowl over there. I really don't ask much from you, Megan, but you didn't even have the respect to let me know you wouldn't be home last night. Now, I have left a poop in my litter tray and I want you to clean that up right away. Then, I would like some fresh food as that stuff has gone stale, and would it kill you to get me a drop of that ice cold milk from the fridge?" Yep, he was pissed alright. We have spent so many years together, I can read his mind. He never stays mad for too long, but I have some sucking up to do later.

My open plan kitchen and living area gives me a sense of freedom. Over the last couple of years, I have developed an irrational fear of closed doors, irrational only from the view of an outsider. Everything is neat and in order. My bookcase consumes an entire wall, arranged alphabetically, starting with *A Beginner's Guide to Black Magic*. I spent days, or even weeks, obsessively making the decision to make the display either alphabetical or chronological. Paintings by my favorite artist, Michael Hussar, take up the remaining wall space throughout.

The rain beats hard against the window pane. I would love to get into my pajamas and sit on the ledge staring the day away until this hangover subsided, but that wasn't an option. My stomach flips a somersault as once again I am reminded of what my day entails. I check the clock, 11:19 am. Time for a shit, a shower and a shave. Oh Megan, you classy girl. I should definitely use that line for today's interview. I burst out laughing at the thought. If only they knew, if only they knew.

The television network has sent a limousine to take me over to the station. I try to play it cool as I greet the driver escorting me under his large black umbrella to my awaiting transport. Inside I am like a giddy child who wants to blurt out, "Oh my God, this is so freaking awesome!

Who else has been in this limo? Is there champagne? Can I choose the music?" But instead I usher a polite and mature observation to the driver, "That's some crazy weather we are having, isn't it?" As I climb into the backseat, the smell of fresh leather fills my nostrils making my head feel a bit fuzzy. I settle in for my very short journey. The butterflies take hold of my stomach once more. I have always found that phrase to be the wrong description. It should be more like 'tigers clawing at your insides' because that's how it feels to me whenever I get nervous.

As we pull up outside the studio, I reluctantly get out. I could have stayed in there all day, feeling like the Queen of Sheba being driven around the city. There is already a strong posse of paparazzi photographers gathered outside and immediately they start snapping their giant cameras in my direction. I am flattered and give them a little wave as we make our way in. My manager, Paul, is waiting in the lobby for me. I immediately throw my arms around him and give him a big hug. This action is a little out of character for me, but it's so reassuring to see a familiar face.

"How ya been, babe?" he says in his typical New York drawl. Normally, I don't like anyone calling me babe, but that's just the way Paul is. It's not said in a sleazy way.

"Oh, I'm okay, a little hungover and a lot of terrified."

"Don't worry about it, you're a natural kid. The minute that camera is in front of you, take a deep breath and do like you always do." With that, he gives a gentle punch to the shoulder.

"This is the next level, Megan. This is the big time. I told you I'd get you here, didn't I?" I try to force my best fake smile to give him the reassurance he is clearly looking for. Paul has been good to me; yes, I am aware that he also makes a lot of money from it, but he has never screwed me over and today is all down to him and his perseverance.

He is old school in his look, slicked back snow white hair tied into a little ponytail, a yellow checkered blazer with the sleeves rolled up, a tad bit tight for his robust figure, and always a cigar in his hand whether it's lit or not. He is also old school in how he handles business; a handshake on a deal with Paul is as good as a legally binding document.

Just as I am starting to relax into the environment, a short girl with bottle top glasses approaches us carrying a clipboard close to her chest. "Hi, my name is Rebecca and I will be taking you down to makeup as soon as you are ready." Rebecca seems stressed, which makes me feel stressed. I say my goodbyes to Paul for now and head off down the long corridors, trying to keep up with Rebecca's frantic paced waddle. When we reach the makeup room, I am greeted by an exuberant guy that goes by the name Tristan. His tall, skinny frame, chiseled cheekbones and bleached blonde hair make him strikingly good looking. He leans in for two cheek air kisses.

"Hey, lovely to meet you girl. Well clearly you are going to make my job very easy today. Just look at that snow white skin, not a blemish to be seen, but hey, if you look good, then I look good." He bursts into a high-pitched laugh at his own little joke, which in turn makes me laugh. I immediately like him and feel comfortable in his presence.

"Okay, so I will be back to get you in a couple of hours. Have fun guys." Rebecca then bolts off down the corridor at lightning speed. Tristan waits until she is out of earshot, "Oh, don't mind her. She has a stress stick firmly lodged up her bum." We both burst out laughing. It feels like I have known him all my life. "Step into my boudoir, madam. We have work to do." The next few hours fly by as we swap stories and antidotes, makeup needing to be reapplied more than once as the tears from my laughter run down my face. I had almost completely forgotten why I was here until a sharp knock rattles on the door and bursts the bubble of our playful banter.

"Hey guys, time to get moving. We all done here?" Rebecca asks in a rhetorical tone. I was sad to be leaving Tristan at this point, but we swap numbers and I will definitely be hitting the town with him some night for cocktails and dancing. "Knock them dead, honey. Oh and make sure you tell them the story of you peeing yourself on Santa Claus's knee in the mall when you were a kid." Once again, he erupts into laughter. This was one of the many stories I had shared with Tristan, but I certainly won't be sharing that one on national TV.

We were off again, making our way down more corridors that seemed to never end. Finally Rebecca stops, "Okay, Megan, here is your dressing room. We will call on you as soon as we are ready. There is bottled water and snacks in the fridge. If you need anything else, just pick up that phone and we will do our best to get it." As soon as I turn around to say thanks, Rebecca was gone.

Being alone was the worst thing at this point as there were no longer any distractions to keep the 'buttertigers' (I have now renamed them) at bay. I look into the full length mirror hanging on the wall to inspect Tristan's work; damn that boy is good at his job. I suddenly feel hugely underdressed and paranoia sets in. Shit Megan, what were you thinking?! Black skinny jeans, Doc Marten boots and a Motley Crew t-shirt that hangs off the shoulder is not exactly the clothing of national TV appearances. I usually dress for comfort over style, but today should have been an exception. Okay, c'mon, let's focus on the positives. Does your hair look good? *Yep, Tristan brushed out the rain frizz and the green hair dye is looking vibrant and shiny.* How about your piercings and tattoos? *Hmm, the new ink from Trent that was done last week is looking so good.*

I had gotten the back of my hand tattooed with a Mandala design done in a pointillism style and I am in love with it. The freshness of the new ink does make my older tattoos look a bit faded and worn in comparison. I have built up quite a collection over the years. Most have direct meanings, a lot are influenced by the bands and music I listen to, and then some I just get because they are pretty (that is a girl's right). One thing that is universal about my tattoos, I will always remember who did them and what point I was at in my life when I got them done. This is my own personal diary, and I hope one day if I am sitting there in my old folks' home that these memories will still bring a smile to my wrinkled face. I check my piercings for any missing attachments. "All good," I reply to the voice in my head that has been asking these checklist questions. Sometimes I think I am losing my mind; sometimes I think it is already lost. I jump as a knock on my dressing room door echoes much louder than a knock should. It is pushed open and Rebecca's little head pokes in. *Damn that bitch is strong,* I think to myself.

"Hi Megan, I'm here to bring you up to the set now."

"Okay, cool," is all I can muster as a response. I am finding it hard to think straight over the noise of my thumping heart ringing in my ears. Suddenly, through the panic, a random movie quote from *Home Alone* pops to the surface – in the words of Kevin McCallister, "This is it. Don't get scared now." My legs feel like lead weights as they trudge behind the ever increasing pace of Rebecca. I wonder if she is getting paid by the step? Before I have time to gather my composure, we have reached our final destination. I can hear the chattering of the live audience from behind the safety of my curtain. Oh, did I mention that this is LIVE? Don't be offended, I have kept it secret from my brain too, until now. And now that my brain has heard this information, it reacts by sending uncontrollable shivers up and down my body. If I stutter, it's live. If I curse, it's live. If my mind goes blank, it's live.

    I try and control the shakes as a runner hooks me up with a microphone. As soon as he has adjusted the wire and does a volume test, the urge to pee washes over me at a dramatic pace. "I'm really sorry, but I have to go pee." He looks unimpressed as he takes my wire back off again. As I carefully line the toilet seat with tissues like I always do to prevent getting 'the cooties', I hum no particular tune to myself, purely born out of nerves. Even after I am done peeing, I sit for an extra thirty seconds. Delaying the inevitable for these precious seconds allows my mind to catch up to form some kind of composure. I feel a huge sense of relief as I make my way back to the set. It would have been a little bit awkward if I had to run to the toilet halfway through the interview.

    Rebecca approaches me, "Oh, there you are. Michael would like to meet you now; come with me." As we cross over to the other side of the set, Michael is getting some final makeup touches done by an overzealous makeup artist. Rebecca approaches with a much softer voice than I have heard from her all day, "Sorry to interrupt, I have Megan here for you to meet."

Michael Corbett is a household name and has interviewed the who's who of the celebrity world over the years. His silver hair compliments his botoxed skin. I feel embarrassed – who the hell was I to warrant a prime time slot with one of the all-time greats of the showbiz industry? I mean, he probably hasn't a clue who I am.

"Megan, how lovely to meet you. My two daughters are huge fans of yours and they have made me promise to get autographs for them." "Aw, really? That's so nice." I am taken aback by his surprising statement. "Oh yes, they never miss a show, and they certainly won't be missing this one." His friendliness and kind words make me feel a lot more relaxed, and for the first time today, I feel like I can actually do this.

CHAPTER TWO

The perspiration leaks from my body at every crevice. The heat from the studio lights burn down deep into my soul. Empty faces in the audience stare back at me. My mouth is dry, but I am too nervous to drink the water laid out next to me. Behind me, there is a huge screen displaying the words 'The Megan Banks Story' highlighted in a lovely gold and black font. The tattoo artist in me takes time to admire the artistic design of the lettering. I shift uncomfortably in my black leather chair, the sweat from my back making me stick to it. *You are one classy lady*, the voice inside my head whispers to me for not the first time today. In front of me, there is an empty chair waiting for the presence of Michael to grace it. Runners and cameramen scurry back and forward as they set up.

A few members of the audience are calling out to me, but it is inaudible, so I just politely smile and wave back. "Megan, Megan, my whole family has just been slaughtered by an axe wielding maniac and now he is here trying to kill me too. Please help!" My imagination runs wild, acting out the scenario. I just smile and wave back at the potential victim that could really be saying anything at all. "We are LIVE in two minutes," comes a voice from somewhere behind me.

"Tristan," I squeal as he appears in front of me for a last minute touch up.

"Hey girl, wow, was Jack Nicholson just here? Because we have *The Shining* happening all over your face." He has me laughing hard once again.

"I know, I am sweating like a fat man at a buffet," I retort through snorted laughter. We are both hysterical with laughter and have to compose ourselves so Tristan can layer on some powder to hide the shine radiating from my face.

"There, much better. That was a close call. Now you go kill it, girl!"

"Thanks, honey," I say with sincerity as he heads off set.

The audience suddenly burst into a round of applause as Michael makes his entrance onto the stage. "Thank you, thank you, lovely to see you all," he says in a charming but professional manner. He makes his way over to me and I am conflicted whether to stand up to greet him or remain seated. *Jesus, Megan, why must you debate every single action in your head?!* Before I have time to answer, I am shaking his hand from my seated position. Oh God, I can feel how clammy my hand is resting in his.

"You all set, Megan? Don't worry, I will take it easy on you," he says with a genuine smile. I watch as he discreetly wipes his sweat filled hand on his suit jacket. I want the ground to swallow me up.

"Yeah, I am a bit nervous but looking forward to it," I lie politely. *Actually, Michael, I am fucking dreading this, was actually thinking of bailing, hitting the nearest bar and getting wasted, you coming?* This response might have been a tad bit out of order.

"Positions everybody." The opening theme music blares out of the speakers. "Michael Corbett presents, *The Megan Banks Story*, live from

New York City." As the music fades out, Michael takes his seat opposite me. The audience applauds enthusiastically until a sign is held up for them to stop.

"Good evening, folks, and thank you for joining us. Tonight, of course, we are here with the gorgeous Megan Banks, tattoo artist and star of the hit reality TV show *Rebel Ink*. Before we get started, let's have a look at this."

With that, the screen behind me kicks into life with a sequence showing clips from *Rebel Ink*, some of the modelling I have done, and also some embarrassing teenage pictures. *Where the hell did they get those pictures?!* I think as I cringe at the sight of them. The audience is all laughing in unison. I have never watched any of my TV show back, so I find it very strange watching this, but I don't want to appear rude by looking away, so I keep my gaze on the screen. I do feel a sense of pride at how professional I look up there. I have accomplished a lot for a twenty-seven year old; my confidence levels begin to rise slowly. As the screen reverts back to the writing, the audience claps and a few hollers of "Go Megan" and "Woo" can be heard.

"Well, just watching that makes me feel extremely bare skinned. I will admit I don't have a single tattoo. I think I'm a bit old now. What do you reckon, Megan?" Okay, this was it, my first sentence; get it right.

"Nah Michael, you are never too old. We can hook you up with a cute little butterfly tattoo." Both Michael and the audience laugh, off to a good start.

"Hmm, we will have to see what Mrs. Corbett has to say about it," he retorts in a jovial manner. "It's gotta hurt though, right?"

This is a question I get asked pretty much on a daily basis. On a normal day it irks me having to repeat the same repetitive answers, but seeing as I am LIVE on a talk show with one of the world's most famous presenters, I will make an exception this time.

"Oh yes, they do hurt. Some places are worse than others, like the ribs and the throat suck to get done, but it's usually always worth the pain for the beautiful artwork you are left with." This is an answer the general public would not get when I am questioned at the checkout in a supermarket.

"I mean, looking at all of your tattoos, you must have gone through some amount of pain. I can hold my hands up and say you are a lot braver than me. Just the sight of a needle and I start to feel light headed." Again, the audience laughs. This is going well, almost too well. *Always the pessimist, Megan.*

"So let me ask you, where did all this start? Take us back to the beginning. Was this always the dream or did your path just lead you to it?" As the words leave his lips, the dread sets back in. Should I tell the real Megan Banks story or the sugar-coated one that I have hidden from all but a chosen few? This is a debate I have had with myself for weeks now. I don't want anybody's pity. As these thoughts race through my mind, I realize I have just been sitting here frozen with a blank expression on my face.

"Are you okay, Megan?" Michael asks in a concerned voice.

"Yes, sorry, I just zoned out there for a minute," I reply as my best defense. I feel my cheeks burn up with the embarrassment.

"Take your time; have a drink of water." I'm sure Michael has producers shouting at him through his earpiece to 'Get her talking again!!!' I take his advice and sip my now room temperature water. Dread, panic, fear, nausea, palpitations – take your pick. Oh, and hello tequila. I see you are still there in the pits of my stomach from last night. Okay, here it goes. I am not really sure which version is going to come out as I begin to speak (at least the speaking part is happening).

"So, I was originally born in Boston. I had a bit of a tough upbringing, but no worse than anybody else's." (This was my first lie. My dad left two weeks before I was born and my mom was a crack addict who brought home multiple partners over the years, some of which abused me physically, emotionally and sexually.)

"I have an older brother," (who is currently serving ten years in a penitentiary for armed robbery). "My dad wasn't around, so it was just myself, my brother and my mom. Unfortunately, my mom died when I was eight years old due to health complications. She was a drug addict." (She died of a heroin overdose and I came home from school to find her lying on the kitchen floor, needle in her arm, her body a marble blue.)

"So myself and my brother were put into foster care, but we were separated. Those years were tough as I was sent from one foster home to another." (Many of the moves were due to the abuse I suffered from my 'foster parents'.) As I spoke, I subconsciously noted that I was giving the sugar-coated version. I had chickened out yet again.

"Art was always my escape from reality. As far back as I can remember, I have always drawn on anything I could get my hands on," (a sharpie was my crack pipe). "When I was thirteen, I won an art competition at the local library. The piece I did was a portrait of a homeless man that used to sit with his dog outside the subway station every day. Thinking back on it now, I suppose it was kind of ironic, as I would find myself living on the streets shortly after." Well done, Megan, that is the first time you have admitted that publicly. I could feel the empathy from the audience as I spoke.

"I would make a few bucks drawing for the kids at school, mainly doing portraits for their family members' birthdays." (I had always felt so jealous drawing these portraits of happy, smiling families. It made me quite sad because I had none of my own.) "The last foster home I was in went bad." (Alcoholic father who beat not only us kids but his wife too – who was vetting these people??!!) "I had had enough and decided to take my chances on the streets. As you can imagine, the streets are not kind to a young girl out on her own." Michael nods his head in agreement. "During the day, I would sit in the park and draw caricatures of passing tourists for ten dollars a pop, and at night I would sleep under the bridge. I picked that spot because even as darkness fell, I could keep drawing under the streetlight above."

"You must have been terrified," Michael interrupts.

"Without sounding cheesy as hell, my drawings kept me company. If I was feeling sad, I would draw something happy. If I was cold, I would draw a tropical paradise, and if I was scared, I would imagine the safest place in the world, and then attempt to draw that too."

"So art pretty much saved your life?"

"Well, now you have just made it sound cheesy, Michael, but yes in a way it really did." (If I was watching me on this program, I would hate me.) I decided to not go into detail about being attacked and robbed, almost dying from hypothermia, and fighting off drug addicts and drug dealers on a daily basis. There are some things just best left unsaid.

"I really had no idea you had it so bad," Michael says with a sympathetic tone.

"No one really does, except for my close friends. It's not something I usually talk about as it is in the past now. I suppose I do feel a little ashamed by it, but you know what? That path defined my future, and if that's what it took to get me to where I am today, then I am totally fine with it now." With that the audience burst into a massive round of applause and I can't help but smile.

Michael waits for the noise to fade out, "That is very true. I am a firm believer in 'everything happens for a reason' and I thank you for sharing that with us tonight." This is the largest scale therapy session I could imagine, but it actually feels good to shed that unwanted skin, like a snake starting afresh.

"So, you are living on the streets of Boston. Tell us how you got out of that situation and ended up here in New York?"

"Okay, so I was now living on the streets for over three years. Occasionally, I got to sleep in friends apartments for a night or two, but there was always drugs being used. I know it sounds ironic, but in a way I am glad I got to see the devastation drugs can cause. I mean, I watched my mother rot from the inside out, and through that I would never touch drugs for as long as I live. Without that knowledge, it would be far too easy to succumb to the temptation. As I used to always say, 'A temporary solution to a permanent problem.' Plus, I was already a little bit crazy, so mixing drugs into that equation would not have ended well." Again, the audience laughs, but I was being serious.

"So anyway, by this stage I was getting pretty well known for my art locally. I had now started selling my portraits and other works of art from my pitch outside the park. Some days, I would go without food, just so I could buy the art supplies that I needed to finish my pieces at night. Even the cops who used to chase me off got to know me. They gave me a break and left me to it. I think the fact that I did a portrait of one particular cop's daughter on the house helped quite a bit. One cold November's day, I am sitting there in my spot doing my thing when I noticed out of the corner of my eye a very fancy looking lady in a mink coat eyeing up my work hanging on the railings. The pearls that hung around her neck were bigger than my hands. I am thinking to myself, 'Wow, this bitch looks loaded. We could be eating well tonight, Megan!!' I stopped drawing and watched as this lady went from painting to painting, spending at least two minutes at a time just staring and tilting her head to the side. 'C'mon lady, hurry up and buy something already.' Finally, she sauntered over to me."

"'Did you do these, my dear?' She spoke with an accent way too posh for Boston. 'Yep, that's my work,' I replied, trying my best not to sound sarcastic. 'It's really rather good.' 'Thank you, would you like to buy one?' I asked quite cheekily. She then let out a little laugh and said, 'Allow me to introduce myself, my dear. I am Lady Miriam, owner of the Nouveau Art Gallery.' Immediately I felt embarrassed that I had not recognized her. I had spent many hours in there studying the work of the world's best artists on display. And how was I to know she was the owner? Because there is a great twenty-foot portrait of Lady Miriam hanging on the wall as you walk in there!!" The audience laughs.

"So now, I had just tried to sell one of my crappy paintings to one of the finest art collectors in the whole country." I feed off the audience's reaction and am feeling more and more confident as my story unfolds. "'Oh, I'm sorry, I didn't recognize you. I am a huge fan of your work,' I replied in a sheepish manner. 'That's quite alright, dear. Now listen to me when I tell you that you have a raw talent and there is honesty in your brush strokes. Next weekend in Nouveau we have an open one-day exhibition for selected artists. Now, usually these artists are well established and work from their cushy studios, but quite frankly these artists bore me, and art should be everything but boring. I didn't happen upon you by chance, my dear. You are creating quite the buzz amongst the people in the know. So, I want you to select your three best works and display them in my exhibition.'"

"I was overwhelmed by her words. Nobody had spoken to me like this before; I was just a nobody. Of course, I knew all about the open exhibition that happens every year, but not in a million years did I ever think my work would ever be good enough for it. I also knew that there was a thousand-dollar retainer fee to enter. So I told her, 'I am honored to be asked, Lady Miriam, but there is just no way that I can afford the retainer fee.' She looked shocked at my response, 'Oh my goodness dear, don't you worry about that. You are my privileged guest. Do you think a lady of my stature would hang around a park in the freezing cold trying to poach artists for a retainer fee?' We both laughed, as she clearly had no problem mocking herself. Before I get to reply, she began to walk away, leaving me with the words, 'No ifs, buts, or maybes, my dear. I will see you this Sunday, nine am sharp.'"

Michael leans forward in his chair looking genuinely interested in my story. "I have actually met Lady Miriam at numerous charity events over the years – wonderful woman and she certainly is a character. So was this the change in direction for you, Megan?" I feel like maybe he is trying to get me back on track. Was I rambling too much? "Yes, it was. Little did I realize at the time, that day my life would change forever. As far as I remember, I don't think I slept for that whole week, staying up all night and painting frantically. I was trying to create something that I felt would be worthy hanging on the walls of Nouveau, but my doubts consumed my brush strokes and the harder I tried, the worse it got. I was actually trying to be somebody I was not, which is completely out of character for me. After a few days working like this, I had given up. I felt like a failure and I sank into a deep depression. For the first time in years, I cried myself to sleep. ('That's it, Megan, you are staying on the streets where you belong.')"

"The next morning, I awoke to the usual sound of shuffling feet making their way to work. I felt so much better after finally getting some sleep. So, with a new burst of confidence, I grabbed my brushes and started to paint again. Without even thinking about it, I began to paint something I had never painted before, my self-portrait. I painted myself sitting in my spot under the bridge, hood pulled tight with the glow of the streetlamp highlighting every shade and tone around me. My brush would not stop. When I am painting from the heart, I am completely entranced and oblivious to everything going on around me. Finally, after some hours, it was done. I stepped back and studied it through squinted eyes. I was proud of it. A huge wave of relief passed over me. It was now Thursday and finally I had a painting I thought was worthy to present to Lady Miriam. Over the next two days, I completed two more. One was a portrait of my street buddy Simon, who stayed up at the other end of the park, and the other one was of a homeless girl named Sally. I asked her to sit outside the Nouveau gallery while I painted her and I paid her whatever I had in my pocket that day. The three paintings had cohesion and I stuck with mainly black and red tones for each of them." Michael nods his head as I continue. I like that he doesn't try to interrupt me as I ramble on, a sign of a good talk show host I think. In all of my sleepless nights worrying about this interview, I had never imagined I would be going into so much detail about my life.

"So anyway, Sunday finally arrives. I packed up my paintings and began the walk down towards Nouveau. As I was walking I felt somebody grab my arm. I turned around and it was a cop. I didn't recognize him as being one of the regular cops that patrolled my area. 'Where you off to?' He had a thick Boston accent. 'Eh, I'm just going to the art gallery, sir,' I replied, feeling a little bit threatened by his tone. 'What's your name, girl?' 'Megan Banks.' 'You got some identification with you?' 'No sir, I don't have my purse with me today. I left it at home.' I knew the drill at this stage, the easiest way was to lie because if you mention you are living on the streets, they want to question you for every crime that has happened that week. 'And where's home then, girl?' I had my friends address memorized for occasions such as this. 'Can I ask what this is about, officer?' 'We have had reports of someone fitting your description selling drugs over at Shelby's.' 'Well you are very much mistaken then; I don't do drugs and I certainly don't sell drugs. Now I am late for my meeting, so I have to go.' I was getting angry now. 'I'm sorry, but I'm going to have to take you down to the station to ask you some further questions.'" I couldn't believe it, my one opportunity to actually do something with my life was now been taken away by being wrongfully pegged as a drug dealer.

This time Michael does interrupt, "That's unbelievable, Megan, so there you are, ready for one of the best things to come your way in a long time, and now this cop is trying to arrest you on the street. What happened?" I can see members of the audience leaning forward intrigued. I hadn't even planned on telling this part of my story at all; it was all just flowing out naturally.

"Well, just as I was thinking the powers of fate had sentenced me to an eternity of doom, it did a three hundred and sixty degree turn. The officer was escorting me to his car as I pleaded with him to let me go, but just as we reached his car, I heard a voice coming from behind us, 'Whatever are you doing, man?' I immediately recognized it; it was Lady Miriam. We both turned around and I will never forget that cop's face when he saw who it was. He looked like a scolded little school boy. 'Josh Turner, is that you?' she asked, in an exasperated tone. 'Yes, Miss Miriam,' he replied in a sheepish response. 'Whatever are you doing to one of my employees?' 'She's wanted for questioning down at the station.' 'Under what charge?' 'Eh I'm not really supposed to say.' With that Lady Miriam shot him a dagger look and he immediately responded,

'For selling illegal narcotics down at Shelby's arcade.' 'And when was this supposed to have happened?' 'Around eight am this morning ma'am.'"

The words were tumbling out of my mouth now. "'Nonsense, Megan was working with me since seven am this morning and the only time she left was ten minutes ago to run an errand for me.' The officer had started to turn a nice shade of crimson red at this stage. 'Now, release my staff at once, young man. We have work to do.' With that he let me go. She told him, 'Tell your mother I was asking for her, Josh, and my, my, you look handsome in that uniform.' The small crowd that had gathered burst out laughing at Lady Miriam's comment and the cop could only mutter a coy, 'Thank you, Miss Miriam.'
She linked my arm as we set off down the street, 'Don't look back, dear, just keep walking.'"

"You have now just incriminated Lady Miriam for aiding and abetting a fugitive on national live TV, but that is amazing." The audience responds to Michael's joke with laughter and applause.

"Ha, well not quite. I was innocent, but she didn't know that, and yet still stuck her neck out for me. I will never forget that for as long as I live, and Lady Miriam if you are watching, I love you." The audience's reactions are like they are watching a sitcom as they 'awwwwwww' in unison. "I even tried to explain myself to her on our walk to the gallery, but she said she didn't need to hear an explanation as she knew I was innocent. She told me that Josh Turner has always wanted to play cop ever since he was a little kid. Turns out she grew up on the same street as his mother and they have been lifelong friends ever since, so yeah, fate was defiantly rooting for me that day."

24

Ink Princess

"As we entered the gallery, the place was already buzzing with excited chatter and clinking of champagne glasses. 'This way, my dear,' she told me. We made our way up the stairs and past the bulging crowd. The gallery is huge, with its naked white walls except for the artwork that adorns it. There is an almost clinical feel to the atmosphere. She told me, 'Here is where you will hang your works, my dear. I will stop by and check on you later.' I was quite surprised as I had thought she would want to see them first, but with that, she shot off to go mingle with her awaiting guests. I hung my three pieces on the hooks that had been set up for me and then remember feeling quite awkward as I really didn't know what to do with myself, so I just pulled up a nearby stool and sat down. Slowly the crowd started to filter through to my area and I was in earshot of their comments. Some of them used words I had never even heard before when describing art like, 'The juxtaposition really speaks to me in this piece,' and 'The appropriation used seems to be a reflection on the artist's life.'"

I was just sitting there praying they wouldn't ask me what any of that means. Overall, the comments and observations all seemed to be positive, which made me happy but also made me uncomfortable as praise made me cringe a little. I remember one guy spending at least twenty minutes studying my paintings and jotting down notes in his flip pad. He had that look of your stereotypical art critic. He wore a haggard brown suede jacket, his thinning hair greasy and slicked back. He chewed on the top of his pencil in between taking notes. I desperately wanted to know what he was writing down. Every time he finished writing, he would stare at me and then back to the painting. I pretended I didn't notice him. This was all foreign to me and I was way out of my comfort zone. I debated leaving, but couldn't do that to Lady Miriam after everything she had done for me. I don't think anyone actually realized I was the artist or one of the protagonists in the paintings, but I was fine with that. And then, the guy that would change the course of my future walked up to study my paintings. And that man was Mr. Lou Marshall." With that, the audience explodes into a rapturous applause at the mere mention of his name. Lou is the owner and head honcho at *Rebel Ink*.

"Really, so that's how you guys actually met? Forgive my naivety, but I just presumed the TV network just kind of put you guys together?" (The shows researcher could be in trouble for this one.)

"Oh no, Michael, we were all friends first, way before the show came along. But yes, that was the first time I met Lou, and you know what? He was the only one who recognized me as the artist. We still laugh about that; in a room full of the best art critics in the country and it's only the leather jacket wearing tattoo artist that makes the link. So, he came up to me and in his typical gravelly voice said, 'Nice work.' Now, I will be honest and say I was very distracted by his tattoos, so I can't really remember what my reply was. I just remember staring at this awesome dragon that ran up the side of his neck. I do remember telling him how cool his tattoos looked, and, yes, it sounded very corny, but he must have taken pity on me because he told me he owned a shop downtown and they were looking for an apprentice. He handed me his card and told me to drop by if I was interested. That card was to be my ticket off the streets."

"And that's why I have 'FATE' tattooed here on my arm. I don't believe in much, but I do believe that everything happens for a reason." (I cringe as I repeat Michael's words from earlier, but he did steal my line.) "If I hadn't of been there that day because that cop had carted me off to the station, if I hadn't been on the streets that day Lady Miriam found me, or if I had let my doubts prevent me from completing the paintings, then I probably would never have met Lou and my story could be an extremely different one than it is today." (A simple flap of a butterfly's wings can change the course of your destiny.)

CHAPTER THREE

"So apparently my paintings had caused quite a stir amongst the art critics and punters in attendance. I remember feeling a tight knot in my stomach as Lady Miriam approached to view my work for the first time. I thought she would hate it."

She told me, 'Well, my dear, I am not always right, but I am never wrong. Art is meant to intrigue, and you have just successfully intrigued your viewers, myself included. Art should provoke questions, and your work here leaves many questions and ponderings about who these people are and how they got here.' She was speaking loud enough for the gathered crowd and reporters to hear. Reporters held out their recorders and exploding flashes boomed from large cameras.
She then said, 'I would like to present to you the future of the art world. This is Megan Banks.'"

"As Lady Miriam gestured towards me, the camera flashes blinded me momentarily and reporters began shouting out inaudible questions all at once. 'Now, now, you vultures back off,' Lady Miriam barked back at them and ushered them back down the stairs. As they slowly left she turned to me and said, 'Always leave them wanting more, my dear.' And she gave me a cheeky wink. I was overwhelmed with what this woman had done for me in such a short amount of time. I am so bad at showing my emotions, so I remember just thanking her and it really came from my heart. She responded, 'No need to thank me, my dear. You are the one with the talent; all I am doing is unveiling it for the world to see.'"

"That's brilliant, she really is a marvelous woman. So, tell us Megan, did you sell the three paintings that day?"

"Well Michael," (I am suddenly self-aware that I am answering his questions using his name to begin my sentence. This is something I never do; why am I doing it now?), "I hadn't even considered the thoughts of selling any. I was just thrilled to even be there, but suddenly the offers came pouring in. One collector even offered twenty thousand for the three. I had never even seen that amount of money in my whole life."

"Lady Miriam called me into her office and said, 'Now, my dear, the wolves are hungry, but if we give them full bellies now, then they will go away and may never return. So, as tempting as it is for you to accept their offers, I implore you to hold back. Once the papers come out tomorrow, you will have hundreds chomping at the bit, and then my dear you can not only name your price, but name your stature in this crazy business.' My head was dizzy with everything that was happening and the voice inside my head was yelling to take the money and run, but I wasn't prepared to ignore the advice from the woman that had gotten me to this position in the first place. I told her she knew best and I will go with whatever she had planned."

"She told me, 'I have been around this game a long time, so you just have to trust me. We will display your work here for a few weeks and then we will have an auction. By then their egos will take over and we will make you some decent money.' I thought to myself, in my world decent money was having a spare twenty bucks to get myself a nice hot meal, but I kept that to myself. She went on, 'Now, my dear, we will be having a little gathering in the Lenox Hotel after this, and I must insist you join me as there will be a lot of people who would like to meet you.' So that night I wined and dined with some of the most elite in the art community. I drank a little too much champagne and chatted the night away with anyone who would listen." The audience let out a little chuckle.

"And was Lou there? Did you get to discuss his offer further?"

"No, he wasn't there – at least I think he wasn't. As I said, I was a little bit drunk that night." I let out a goofy laugh, one that I had promised myself I would try and contain tonight, but everyone laughs with me, so it makes it slightly less awkward. "It is probably a good thing that he wasn't there. If he had met drunk Megan that night, then he might not have given me the shot that he did."

"So this day literally changed your life. Tell me, what happened next?" Once again, I think he is getting me to focus and get on with it. *Jesus, Megan, you do ramble on sometimes, and this isn't the place to be doing it.* It's like word vomit and I can't keep it down!

"With the offer from Lou consuming my thoughts, I made sure I was there outside Rebel Ink on the Monday morning. As it turns out, 8am might have been a bit hasty, as I now know us tattoo artists like to sleep in a bit. The shop opened at 11 am. I have never felt so nervous in my entire life, even doing this show wasn't as bad, Michael."

As he throws his head back with laughter, I take time to ponder whether those pearly white gnashers are his own or some fine orthodontic work. *Concentrate Megan!*

"So there I was, sitting up against the shutters, when a tall, handsome man strolled up with keys in his hand – that man was, of course, Zane Norton." The audience claps loudly as they all know Zane as the shop manager from the show. I can't help but smile with pride. Zane is one of my closest friends and such a genuinely nice guy. "I remember him saying to me, 'Sorry hun, we don't open for another hour yet. Is there anything I can help you with?' I rather sheepishly replied, 'Emm, I was speaking to Lou over the weekend and he told me to drop by for a possible apprentice position.' 'Oh, okay, cool, you can come on in and wait while I get set up if you like.'"

"So, I waited for an hour watching Zane set up the shop with his usual attention to detail that I have now grown to love. You guys have to know something about Zane; I can tell you first hand that what you see is what you get. The way he is on the show is exactly how he is in real life; there is no bullshit with that man. I really don't know where he gets all his energy and positivity from, but if we were all half the person he is, then this world would be a better place." As soon as the words leave my mouth, something unusual happens. The usual tough as nails Megan felt a large lump come to her throat and tears filled my eyes. I just felt so emotional about what I had just said, it overwhelmed me for a moment.

"Are you okay, Megan? Would you like a tissue?" Michael asked with sincerity in his voice.

"Ha sorry, I'm really not usually a crier. It's just Zane has done so much for me, and he has such a kind heart. I got a little overwhelmed speaking about him there. Oh God, I am never going to live this one down with the guys at the shop. They already give us hell for being like two peas in a pod."

"Don't you worry about those guys. If they are giving you hassle, you tell them to come and see me. Just make sure my security are around when you do." *Thank you for saving that awkward moment with your little joke, Michael*, I think as I wipe the tears from my eyes.

"So anyway, Lou eventually shows up and Zane points over to me and says, 'This girl Megan is here to see you, Lou.' He strolls over and says in his gravelly voice, 'Hey Megan, so what are you thinking about getting done?' I nearly died. He had forgotten me and thought I was there to book a tattoo."

Michael throws his hand to his head, "Oh how embarrassing," he says, with no real need to point out the obvious.

"I know, it was not the best of starts," I reply in a humorous tone. "So I told him, 'Emm, sorry I'm not actually here for a tattoo. I'm the girl from the art exhibition. You told me to come see you about a possible apprenticeship here at the shop.' He replied, 'Oh shit, Megan! I'm so sorry, I am terrible with faces; don't take any offence.' He turned to Zane and said, 'Thanks for letting me walk into that one, Dipshit" "Hey, don't blame me because your old man-ass, can't remember what he had for breakfast that morning!' As you guys know from the show, these guys rib on each other like this on a daily basis, but beneath it all they really love each other. You can't be too sensitive if you want to work in our shop, that's for sure. But yeah, that's how my first proper encounter went down with Lou and I still give him crap over it to this day. Over the years I have learned that man has no facial recognition capacity whatsoever, so it wasn't just me, which is quite a relief."

"Brilliant, this is exactly why we are doing this show, to get the inside scoop on these characters that have become worldwide sensations, and of course you are included in that, Megan. We are eager to learn more, but right now we have to take a short commercial break. Come back and join us to find out more about this fascinating young lady and her rise to be one of the world's best tattoo artists and TV star sensations."

As the music starts back up, I can finally relax my body from the tense posture I have maintained during the course of the interview. "Absolutely brilliant stuff, Megan. How are you feeling?"

"Aww, thanks Michael. I'm an emotional wreck and have no idea what I have just said in the last half an hour. I am so sorry for rambling on."

"Not at all, you are doing great, the more detail the better. According to the voice in my ear, our social media pages are crashing due to the response from people watching at home."

"Really? Well, you are making it so much easier for me. Thank you for being so kind." I have to admit, hearing people were responding positively made my confidence rise a little bit and I regain my composure. Tristan runs on to the stage, and starts fixing my makeup frantically. "Oh girl, you are just killing it. My phone has been hotter than a fireman at a Lady Gaga concert. They all want me to get pictures for them backstage after the show."

"Oh, anything for you, my dear," I reply, feeling a bit embarrassed again. As he empties half a bottle of hairspray on my head and dabs the shine off my forehead, he looks me straight in the eye and says, "You look a million dollars. I can only take credit for half of that million, the other half is all you, honey. Now, if somebody wants to pay me that amount, then who am I to say no?" Once again, he has me laughing at his wacky personality and snappy one liners as he runs off backstage. Michael returns to his seat and the runner informs us that we are back on air in two minutes.

"You ready to rock again, Megan?"

"Ah sure, I'm here now; might as well do it, Michael." My attempt at a joke is born out of my returning nerves setting back in.

"Welcome back folks. So, as you know, tonight's show is about a talented young lady named Megan Banks. We all know her from the five series, multi-award winning TV show *Rebel Ink*. But tonight we are finding out so much more about her amazing story and rise to the top. It's a real classic rags to riches story and it has clearly touched the hearts of people across the world. Our Twitter page has had thousands of you respond already, and if you would like to add anything, you can tweet us here at #themeganbanksstory."

"So Megan, where were we before the forces of the commercial world so rudely interrupted us? Ah yes, you had just met your mentor to be, and he had quite awkwardly not remembered who you were. Sorry to bring that back up again, but it is quite amusing. Hopefully it got better

Ink Princess

from there?" "That's okay, Michael, I am glad the world knows now, but yes, fortunately it did. Lou took me up to the office and we had a long chat about my art and what exactly a tattoo apprenticeship would entail. He never once asked about my background or anything like that. It was purely focused on the art and making sure I was fully committed. Lou has been in this game a long time and has seen many people come and go. He was not prepared to waste his time with somebody he didn't feel was 100% committed."

"I remember him saying to me that day, 'This is no easy ticket. We are old school in our apprenticeships here. The title of a tattoo artist has to be earned and not just given. Having the artistic talent that you possess is only 50% of what you need to make it in this game. I know plenty of amazing artists that have tried and failed to become true tattoo artists. Working on the skin is a whole new medium, and unlike anything you have experienced before. Working on a human being, there is no room for error, no eraser you can reach for to undo any mistakes. The mental pressure is what breaks most in this game. some try to mask it with drink and drugs, but the true artists have no doubt in their minds when they pierce the skin with that needle. And if you make it that far, you will also have no doubts. Work ethic cannot be taught; either you have the drive to succeed or you don't. I am not here to force you to do anything, but if you are not doing the things needed to better yourself as an artist, then you will be not a part of this shop. It may sound harsh, but I will not let anybody drag this shop down in any way. If you succeed, then you are a part of this family and you will remain that way for as long as you want it. We are a tight bunch here and they may be hard on you to test your willingness and your want for this position, but don't ever take it personally. This is not just their job, this is their life and they are very protective of who they let in. So after hearing all of that, do you still want the position?'"

"Of course, I told him I wanted it and wouldn't let him down. In an age where tattooing has become so mainstream, there are so many people jumping on the bandwagon for all the wrong reasons. They think it's a fast route to a rock and roll lifestyle. It really couldn't be further than the truth. The true artists work their asses off to give the client the tattoo that both the artist and the client can be proud of. Although it may seem harsh to some people, Lou is protecting the industry he loves by not just teaching his skills to somebody that is doing it for the wrong reasons. I always say, there is a huge difference between a 'tattooist' and a 'tattoo artist'. The tattooist does it mainly for the money and has a basic skill level to just get by. The work is usually mediocre and often they have no formal training, they really don't care about the tattoo they are putting on somebody for life. In contrast, a tattoo artist puts as much time, effort, and passion into a tattoo that he would for a piece of art on canvas that he was displaying in an exhibition. They are an artist first and respect the industry. You need to understand how to design a piece to make it flow with the shape of the client's body. Shading understanding and technique can make or break a tattoo, and knowing your color palette is vital."

"It really boils my blood when I see these hacks dragging the industry down with crap tattoos and it is very clear they just went and bought a machine off eBay and thought they would skip the hard bit and just give it a go to make a couple of bucks. In the long run, these hacks rarely last, but unfortunately it is then up to us to fix up their mess and also to fix up the bad reputation they give the tattoo world. The only way to stop these guys is for the public to just not let them mark their bodies. There really is no excuse these days to not research a professional artist; check their portfolio and references and make sure they are the right artist for you. If somebody is tattooing from their kitchen, there is a reason for this. I mean, would you go to a plastic surgeon that worked from their kitchen? Of course not. If you are doing it because it's the cheaper option, then you really need to reconsider your priorities. You cannot put a price on taking a risk with your body. One of my favorite sayings we have at the shop is, 'Good tattoos aren't cheap, and cheap tattoos aren't good. If in doubt, wait it out.'"

As I pause for a breath, the audience claps and cheers louder than they have all night. "Well said, Megan, this is something you are clearly passionate about."

"Yes, it really is, and apologies for the rant and going off topic, but it is a major problem right now that is having a huge negative effect on the industry. You know, TV shows like ours are great for educating people to the possibilities of what can be achieved in a tattoo, but I also worry that some people are watching and don't see how hard it actually is to get to that position and are picking up machines thinking it's an easy gig. Unfortunately, they are causing so much damage, it's setting us back ten years again. So just to end this rant, if you really want to be a tattoo artist, please ensure you seek out the best environment and do a proper apprenticeship. And if you are getting a tattoo, make sure you go to a professional who is certified and ask to see their portfolio first."

As the audience claps, I am content in the knowledge that it was the first proper thing I had said during this whole interview and took full advantage of getting my point across to this captive audience. I am sure it will be appreciated by tattoo artists across the world.

"Some great advice to follow there, folks, if you are considering getting a tattoo. Frankly, I am a little shocked that this is actually going on; to be honest, I had no idea. It will be something I will be having a word with my girls about it as they are getting to the age of wanting a tattoo."

"Send them to me, Michael. I will be sure to give them a good deal."

"I will hold you that," he says with his finger pointed and eyebrow raised in a serious enough manner to make it seem like a real statement.

I wonder if the guys from the shop were watching this; I hope I am doing them proud. Even after all these years, I still seek and crave their approval. I don't think that feeling will ever change and, to be honest, I don't really want it to.

"Okay, so you have now landed yourself an apprenticeship. Tell us, was it as hard as Lou had spoken about and how did you fit in with the guys at the shop?"

"My journey started right after my conversation with Lou and I was thrown straight into it. I was told to shadow Zane for the day and he would start showing me the ropes. This is when I first met the members of my new family. As with any family, everyone has their role to play in making it function; personalities are diverse, but the foundation of any family is love, and once you have that, it works. So we have Lou, who is the father figure of the shop; Zane is like the older brother who looks after everybody; Mike Verges is the fun uncle everyone wants around; Trent is the middle child—yes, he's moody and short tempered but he will do anything for his family, and that dude has a wicked sense of humor once you get to know him. Our piercer, Frankie Boy, is like all the best cousins combined into one, loves to party but loves his work even more. Me? I suppose I would be the annoying little sister, always nagging and making sure everybody is getting along. Sadly, as you know, a member of our family is no longer with us. Sammy was killed in a car crash in 2012 and it was the hardest thing to come to terms with. It still is. As much as Sammy would kill me for saying it, he was the mother figure of the shop. He was always the one we went to with our problems and whenever he talked, you would listen. He was the smartest man I had ever known and his absence leaves a hole in my heart." They must have been planning on asking me about Sammy's death as I catch an image of him smiling up on the screen behind us.

"We were all very saddened to hear of his passing. I mean, we knew him from the TV show and he certainly was a talented tattoo artist, but you knew him, as you say, as a part of your family. After his death, was there any doubts about continuing the show?" His words are blurred as my eyes are transfixed on the screen. The face that I miss so much, smiling as he so often did. He was a naturally rugged, good looking guy, messy bed head with a permanent 5pm beard shadow. His black and grey tattoos complimented his features, and he was always a big hit with the ladies. I am aware of my pause in answering Michael's question, but in that moment I didn't really care. Eventually my thoughts come around to reach my mouth.

"You know, that's not what Sammy would have wanted. He was so passionate about our shop and about the show. Don't get me wrong, it was tough and there were definitely doubts and low morale surrounding the future of *Rebel Ink*. I think Lou took it the hardest as they have known each other since they were kids and they supported each other through thick and thin. If anything good came out of Sammy's death, I suppose it would be that it gave us a kick up the ass. Life can be taken away as quick as his was that night, and all the trivial crap seemed pathetic in the grand scheme of things. I have his portrait here on my leg to remind me of the happy years we spent together." I lift up my jeans to show my incredible portrait that Lou did for me.

"I can tell you all now, Lou is not one to suffer from nerves when it comes to tattooing, but by God, he was nervous doing this one that day. He said if he messes this one up, Sammy would come back and kick his ass!! But he nailed it, and I know Sammy would be proud of him." I didn't really want to talk about it anymore and Michael, being the experienced host he is, senses it and moves on.

"So how long did it take for you to actually do your first tattoo?"

"Sorry, to answer your original question, it was tough going through the apprenticeship, but I was supported the whole way. That first day in the shop, Lou had just finished his last customer and I was packing up getting ready to leave. He asked me how the day went and then said to me that if I was to be fully committed I would have to take the room upstairs to live in as he needs me there full time. I now know that he knew of my living situation and it was his way of being kind to me. He knew if he had just offered it to me I would have said no as I didn't want charity – he was right. That was a huge turning point for me. I now had a focus and a determination to make it work. It was almost a full year before I would do my first tattoo on human skin – a lot of poor deceased pig skins were adorned with some incredibly bad tattoos over that year though. I had to learn all about cross contamination, blood borne pathogens, aseptic technique and sterilization before I was allowed near any of the equipment. I drew until my hands were blistered and numb. I cleaned until my mind was blistered and numb. Seven days a week."

"Living upstairs in the shop, I hardly had any excuses not to show up. Zane taught me the counter side of things and I worked alongside him soaking up his fountain of knowledge. I got to sit and observe the guys working their magic on customer's skin and I annoyed them with a barrage of questions as they did so. I lived and breathed the shop until it ran through the blood in my veins. In a way, I became obsessed with it. I'm sure if you asked a therapist they would tell you I had used the shop to fill the void left from my family's abandonment of me. This is probably true, but it was the first time I had felt I belonged and I wasn't going to throw it away. Living in a building again really took some getting used to. It was nice to have my own bed, to be warm and feel safe. Having a shower all to myself was my own personal lottery win. The main thing that I struggled to get used to was the silence. I had become so accustomed to the murmur of traffic and the hustle bustle of the active city that the silence was foreign to me. I suppose it was post traumatic homeless syndrome."

I finally take a pause, as again I feel like I am rambling on and not sure if I am giving the right answers to these short open ended questions that Michael was asking. Why or who thought it would be a good idea to have this going out live? No time for editing. No control over what I say or how I say it. This is dangerous, both for me and for them...

Diary Entry:

My face is perished from the cold. Wind howling around every corner, consuming its victims and making them squint down hard, distorting faces. Definitions of a scowl. Businessmen pull large collared jackets tight around their necks. Their hands protected by leather bound gloves. Snowflakes dance in the air, threatening to stick but never spending long enough to do so. Faint echoes of carol singers are carried to my frozen ear drums by the wind. Horse carriages carrying cargos of happy families clip clop by. Even the horses are clad in storm bearing jackets, insulating the heat carried in their mass of blubber. Pull my knees in tight. Rocking back and forth to maintain any form of circulation flow to thaw my veins. Eyelids stick a little with each blink, eyes water, eyes dry out. There is no rapid eye movement tonight. My body aches to sleep, but every attempt is thwarted by the pain. No pictures drawn of tropical sunsets can save me from this tonight. Holding this pen makes my fingertips sting as I write. My mind is in automatic survival mode. It barks orders and whispers suggestions. Go find a pub, where there is warmth. Go knock on those offered doors you have refused.

Go to the shelter. Go to sleep, Megan. This will all go away and everything will be okay. But I don't move. I daren't move. There is not a lot I can be grateful for right now, but the hat pulled down to eye level is my savior. I convince my fragile mind that without this hat, tonight I would be dead. A woolen cross stitched green hat (in my mind) is the difference between a human being surviving a night on the streets or succumbing to the elements, paying the price with your life. I don't want to check the time as to put a time on this misery would surely break what is left of my morale. Derelict or destitute, take your pick. I keep my head down. I don't want to catch sympathy in eyes,

Ink Princess

at the same time I don't want to see them ignore. 'Dirty little junkie, serves her right.' My usually fluorescent street lamp is now hazy and flickering as the snow spills down at a diagonal slope. I never left anything down around me that would suggest I am begging for people's 'spare' pieces of paper. Get me, a girl sitting on the cold concrete in a blizzard and still holding on to ideals of pride by not accepting strangers' pity money. 'Your pride will get you killed, you stupid girl.'

    I normally keep the demons at bay, but tonight they are clawing and creeping their way in. I begin to feel sorry for myself and despise myself for doing so. The chattering voices of merriment now irk me. I feel rejected by the world. It's a cliché for the misfortunate of the world to feel depressed during this season, but tonight it just hurts that bit more. If I believed in God, I would be angry at him right now, dare him to smite me, taunt him with, 'That all you got?' Maybe, if I believed in God, I wouldn't be sitting here right now. But, my ever-questioning independent mind would never allow belief in the big ghost in the sky, controlling us all like puppets on a string. Followers, following fables. Myths and stories written to scare 'man' into behaving; a threat of impending doom awaits those who disobey our man made rules. I have always rebelled from any form of control, so I could never find solace in a man dressed in black preaching words of a mythical being that neither he nor I had any proof existed. I was always quite envious of people who could blindly follow their God, and whose minds were put at ease to any ruptured event that happened through their life, putting it down to 'An act of God' or 'God's will'. Maybe I was being punished for not being part of the flock, maybe this is my penance. "Repent, and thou shalt be saved," I mutter sarcastically to myself. As my self-pity and life evaluation turns to anger, I am snapped out of my thoughts by a voice. Not one from the distant murmurs from the passing crowds; this voice is directed at me. Has 'God' sent me an angel after hearing my cries of non-believer? Not quite (or maybe). A rosy cheeked little girl is standing in front of me. She can be no more than eight years old. Her eyes filled with concern, the kind of concern I usually did not want to see in strangers' faces. But this was too cute to be dismayed by, her red duffle pea coat buttoned to the top just covering the chin of her milky white face and a hat sporting some form of blue monster plonked over her head.

"Hi, my name is Sonya and my mom told me to give you this." She looks pleased with herself, that she has successfully got the obvious rehearsed sentence out in one go. She then hands me a white Styrofoam cup. I struggle to lift my arms from their anchored position, but slowly my hands meet the heat that is emulating from the liquid inside. Sonya then does a small twirl from side to side with her feet stationary. She smiles with the satisfaction that I have accepted her gift, her smile displaying a glorious gap from where her baby front teeth used to be. As I move my lips to speak, there is no audible sound coming out. As I muster the energy for a second attempt, Sonya runs off. My heart sinks as I wanted so desperately to thank her and ask her what 'Santa Claus' was bringing her tonight (Santa Claus falling into the category of mythical stories, only this one is made up for kids, and adults believing in that sort of nonsense would be mocked, right?). The heat from the cup is thawing the numb out of my bitter hands clasped around it. I didn't want to drink from it right away, just bask in its warmth for a moment.

"And this." It was Sonya back again. This time standing to my side, her arm outstretched holding a large pretzel. As I look up to meet her second gift, I spot 'Mom' standing back along the railings. She looks proud of her daughter as she gestures to me, her arms laden down with various shopping bags. I nod my head in recognition but not noticeably because I would hate to spoil Sonya's big moment. Finally my words come out, "Aww, thank you sweetie. I just love pretzels." My tone is as close as I can get when speaking with an eight year old. She giggles and replies, "Me too," and takes a scoot back over at Mom to make sure it is ok to reply to the girl sitting on the ground.

"Now, what is Santa Claus bringing you tonight?" I ask with as much enthusiasm as possible.

"Ehh, a purple bike with sparkles, a Mr. Snow dump truck and a Tinkerbell fairy castle," she lists off with ease as this has clearly been repeated over the last few weeks.

"Oh, how lovely, you must have been a very good girl to be getting such lovely gifts." There's that smile again.

"Are you cold?" she asks with concern on her delicate face.

"Who, me? No, I'm not cold. Look, I have a nice cozy hat on just like you." Her little gloved hands reach up to check if her hat is indeed still on her head. I can see her little mind racing now, conducting her next question.

"Is Santa going to visit you tonight?"

"Well, I hope he is." Sonya, it would seem, is going to make one heck of a journalist, as it becomes clear that her first question was just a gateway to the real question that she wanted to know the answer to.

"But how will he find you out here?" I can't help but push my bottom lip up to make the 'sad puppy face' at her innocence and cuteness. Before I have a chance to reply with some made up reassurance that the big man in the sky (not that one - the other one, with the red suit) knows where I am and will surely find me, she is beckoned back to her awaiting mother. As Sonya literates the story of what just happened back to her mom, her head bobbing with excitement, I mouth the words

'Thank you' over to her and she accordingly mouths back 'You are welcome.'

As I take my first sip of the bitter coffee (I am not in a position to complain about the lack of sugar), my body unclenches for the first time in hours. I gnaw on the pretzel like a hamster, my frozen muscles not up to full strength yet. This small act of kindness and the form it came in (Sonya) has momentarily restored my faith (fate) in humanity. Was this an act of God? Was this an act of Santa Claus? Whatever it was, I needed it. As my eyes close and I drift off to sleep, I just hope that he does find me.

Christmas Eve. 2006.

CHAPTER FOUR

My palpitations have finally begun to subside. My body is luring me into a false sense of security, but I am happy to comply.

"Your style of tattooing is quite bold and colorful; was it always that way?" As Michael says the words, a perfectly timed slideshow of my work begins on the screen behind us. Always my own worst critic, I look away instantly.

"You know, it's funny, my artwork has always had a realism feel to it, quite dark. Lou took me out of my comfort zone and during my apprenticeship he made me try every single aspect and style of tattooing. As he always says, a good tattoo artist will always have a trademark style, but first you must make sure to at least try all styles to make sure they aren't right for you. An artist should always be evolving, pushing the boundaries. If an artist becomes stale, then it shows through their work. So, as I began to explore these various styles, I found myself drawn to the 'New School' style of tattooing, which is something I had never even tried before. It was so exciting to suddenly be drawing in a completely different way after so many years thinking I had reached my limits."

I continued, "Our shop is a true drawing shop; we all bounce off one another and help and guide as much as we can. Any of those guys could stand alone as artists if they weren't putting it on people's skin. The style of 'New School' tattooing could be described as a twist on the 'Traditional' or 'Old School' style. Bold, solid lines, but with saturated color in bright, vibrant tones. I just love how striking this style of tattooing looks on the skin. Its thick lines and solid color hold up really well over the years for the wearer. I still love doing portraits and try to incorporate this style into them wherever I can. As you can see, my cute animal portraits are definitely one of my favorite things to do."

"Well, if Mrs. Corbett had her way, I would be getting a portrait of our prized pooch from you, Megan, but I just don't think I could pull off having a cute little Labradoodle on my arm. I mean, I would surely lose all of my street cred."

"Yeah, you could be right," I reply, fighting the urge to go on the defensive about getting a tattoo for yourself, not for other people to judge.

"So let's go back. You are working your way through your apprenticeship and things have really turned around for you. At this stage you have no idea what's going to happen with the show, right?"

"Oh God no, I was just so happy to have the opportunity given to me and I was working hard. After my first two months being in the shop, the guys would pay me some cash to draw up their stencils and they would always share tips. Some of you may not know that proper apprenticeships are not paid, and actually the norm is for you to pay the shop for teaching you. Lou never asked me for any money nor did we ever discuss it. I mean I had a roof over my head and was learning my craft from the best in the business, so as long as I had money for food, I was happy. Then one day Zane came into the back and said there was a lady out front looking to speak with me. At this stage I hadn't any customers and no one really knew I was there, so I was apprehensive. Paranoid it was the authorities (always my first assumption from years of dealing with them), I hesitantly poked my head out to try and get a glimpse of who it was. To my relief, it was Lady Miriam. I had only been back once to see her after the exhibition as I was so busy with the shop. She was delighted I had found my feet but also disappointed as she had offered me a position as a curator in her gallery. (This offer was definitely out of sympathy, as there was no need for any more staff, nor did I have the qualifications required. I still appreciated the gesture, but was also glad I was in a position to turn it down). I had strangely missed her even though our encounters were brief. I suppose, in a way, she was the closest mother figure I had in my life since my real mother had died."

"She said to me, 'Hello my dear, I promised you I would drop by, didn't I?" as she kissed me on each cheek. 'I'm so glad to see you,' I replied hopefully sounding genuine. We chatted for a bit, like two old friends catching up and getting the compulsory niceties out of the way. 'So dear, I have something for you,' she said and she reached into her crystal white Prada bag and produced a folded piece of paper and ushered it towards me. I have to admit when I unfolded it, my legs shook a little and a wave of excited nausea shot through my body. It was a check. Made out to me for $65,000. My mouth wide open, Lady Miriam smiled warmly and said, 'You have earned every cent, my dear.' This was clearly not true as she had done all the groundwork of selling my paintings on my behalf at auction. I told her, 'I really don't know what to say. Surely half of this money belongs to you.' She responded, 'Don't be silly, my dear. That is your money; do with it as you please. I am rewarded enough with the confirmation that I was right to hold out for the blood thirsty sharks to take a bigger bite.' Then, I remember making her laugh like I had never heard her laugh before when I sheepishly said, 'But I don't even have a bank account.' She reached out her perfectly manicured hand and placed it on my forearm and said, 'Don't worry dear, once you walk in there holding that check, they will do all they can to get you signed up with them.' So she left me, my body still shaking. I think flabbergasted would be the right description as to how I was feeling at that moment."

"That's amazing, Megan, and not to belittle your work or anything, but those same three pieces you probably would have sold from your pitch at the park for what, maybe $60?"

"Oh more like $30," I reply, trying to sound modest.

"The art business has always baffled me, but there you go, proof that if it's portrayed to the right people, then you can make the money your talent deserves. So, that must have helped you immensely in pushing on with your career?"

"It really did. I mean, I had nothing, and then to suddenly have this cash behind me I could finally get the things I needed, and also (for the first time) the things I wanted. And you know what? I tried to give Lou some rent money towards my bills for staying there, but he would not take a dime. Same with the guys at the shop. They had helped me out so much I wanted to pay it back to them, but they point blank refused to accept anything. So one night, when they all went home, I bought a new sound system for the shop and spent all night hooking it up. Our one was on its last legs and I knew Lou was saving to get a new one. It was just my small way of saying thank you to them. After that, I splashed out on the top of the range art supplies. I had always dreamed of buying my own personal light box for late night drawing in my room, and now I had the money to make it a reality." (I also made sure to seek out Simon and Sally and present them with cash for posing for me, and five years later I donated $1.2 million to the Boston homeless shelter. I remained anonymous then, and I want to keep it that way now.)

I always wondered afterwards if the person who had bought my paintings knew what happiness the money had brought me. I can never thank them as I don't know who bought them, but I am forever grateful." The audience claps at my heart warming tale of the kid off the street getting some well-deserved karma her way.

"I love it. Okay, so your first tattoo you did on skin, who was the brave candidate? Because that must be a scary process for both involved."

"Oh, well, that brave candidate was actually me, Michael."

He makes an ouch motion with his lips pursed, "Really, you tattooed yourself?"

"Yep, that is definitely a rite of passage when you are an apprentice. Your first tattoo should be on yourself with your mentor watching over you."

"So, c'mon tell us, what did you do and was it any good?"
With that, I stand up and roll my tight skinny jeans up over my right knee, struggling as they are stuck with sweat (sexy, eh?). "This is it here, a

traditional lighthouse." The camera zooms in and it appears up on the big screen.

"Now, I'm no expert but that looks pretty darn good to me, folks." They clap (hopefully) in agreement.

"I later added the Rebel Ink logo around it. It may not be perfect, but I won't touch it as I want it as a reminder of where it all began."

"Well yes, that's the great thing about tattoos. They are set as landmarks or reminders of people's lives, and are often used as memorials to lost loved ones, which in a way is the ultimate tribute." (I appreciate him making an effort, although I'm not entirely convinced he actually feels this way. The sceptic in me believes he may have read this somewhere while prepping for the show.)

"Yeah, I guess it's your own personal permanent journal." I say it more to support his efforts of relating to the tattoo world than any further meaning. "So, that was my first one, and, yes, I was terrified doing it, but my next tattoo was even more terrifying to do; it was on Lou." The audience return to their sitcom traits as they 'ohhhhhh' and 'ahhhhh' and then burst into laughter once again.

"No way, no pressure then? What did you do on him?" Michael asks, keeping up the pantomime tone of it all.

"As you probably already know, Lou is a huge Red Sox fan, so I did their logo on his leg. Of course I was nervous, but as I said earlier, Lou wouldn't have let me do it unless he knew I was fully confident that I could pull it off. I think he was happy with it when I was finished. Well, he didn't kick my ass, so I took that as a good sign."

I catch a glimpse of Paul's silhouette through the blinding stage lights for the first time. I squint hard to make out that he is giving me a vigorous thumbs up. I quickly relax my face – not a good look on LIVE TV, Megan!!!!

"Okay, so you have your first two tattoos under your belt. How long was it before you were working on clients and building a name for yourself?"

"Honestly, from those first two tattoos it was full steam ahead. I had built up a good rapport with the guys' customers while sitting in on their sessions. So by that stage they all knew I was doing my apprenticeship and a lot of them offered up their skin for when I was ready. When the word got out that I was ready to start tattooing, I actually got booked up really fast with willing candidates (not too hard when the tattoos were for free). Again, the guys at the shop were all amazing and took me through each tattoo step by step. You know, Trent was probably the toughest on me out of all the guys during that time, but he just wanted to make sure I was as committed as I needed to be and made sure each piece I did was good enough to be coming out of the shop. These guys had spent years and years building up the reputation they had, so I understood them wanting to protect it."

"In those early days, I just did whatever the customer wanted. Just as Lou had wanted, I got to do every possible style there is, tribal, old school, realism pointillism, traditional, neo traditional, geometric, etc., etc. After about a year of this, I finally got to do my first portrait tattoo. I reveled in the challenge and spent weeks drawing and redrawing the piece until I was sure it was right. As any artist will tell you when it comes to a portrait tattoo, if you get one little line wrong, the whole piece can be ruined in an instant (this mainly applies to the 'tattooists' I mentioned earlier. They can try to bullshit their way out of other styles, but there is just no hiding from a bad portrait. Just hit Google search if you want the evidence). There is no escaping from realism. You have the photograph of the person or animal right there in front of you and if you can't translate that exactly onto skin, then you are in big trouble. My first portrait was of a guy's twin sister. The photo he brought in was of her when she was like five or six. He wanted it in black and grey, which works really well with portraits. Mike Verges, who is an amazing portrait artist in his own right, stood over me the whole way through, and his advice was so reassuring and helped me nail it. He even claims that I taught him a thing or two, with my use of white highlights in the eyes, but I think he was just trying to make me feel good. So yeah, once that piece went up on the shop's website, things really started to take off for me."

"It must be a tremendous amount of pressure doing a portrait for a client that has lost a loved one?"

"You have no idea how scary it is. It is such a personal thing getting a portrait done of a deceased loved one, and it is up to you, the artist, to give them an accurate representation through ink. Often the client can be quite emotional about it, as you have seen on our show, and you have to be sympathetic, but at the same time not lose focus on the piece you are doing. This can be quite difficult to find the right balance." This is putting it lightly. In many cases you become a counsellor. Not many people realize what a mentally draining job being a tattoo artist is.

All of your focus and energy is devoted to the piece you are working on for hours at a time. It leaves you emotionally drained at the end of the day (this is why, unfortunately, a lot of tattoo artists turn to drinking and drugs to deal with it, also a recurring fact with high pressure jobs like pilots, surgeons and cops). But when you throw in a tragic circumstance behind the meaning of the tattoo, it makes the stress levels triple, and it can leave you feeling burnt out fast. I leave this part out of my answer because I don't want to seem negative or whiney towards our customers or make a broadcast statement that a lot of tattoo artists turn to narcotics to deal with the pressure. Enough of them resent me anyway, so that would just add fuel to the ever burning fire.

"Yes, we certainly see some amazingly heartfelt stories on the show. It must make you feel good getting to help these people get through tragic circumstances by giving them a tattoo?"

I hesitate to answer this as I have to hold back my real feelings on it, my 'truth' answer. Yes, it is nice to help people to get through tough times in their life, but... and don't judge me on this...

1. I am getting paid for this, so don't claim me as some Good Samaritan doing it for the sole purpose of 'helping them'.
2. Not all tattoos HAVE to have a meaning behind them. The TV show is portrayed this way as it increases ratings. (Everyone loves a sob story, right?) This aspect has always made me feel like a sellout, but I have had to bite my tongue about it (like I am doing right now).

3. Most people don't realize the clients on the show have to fill out an application form explaining the reason for the tattoo they want to get (the more tragic the better) to even be considered by the powers that be.

4. If there is a genuine reason behind the tattoo, then that is absolutely fine, but this whole 'forced reason' just to make an entertaining show is totally unnecessary. So, you will see something as ornate as a flower being tattooed on someone on the show, and they're all like 'Yeah, so this is to represent my goldfish that died tragically when I was 10.' No, you are getting this flower tattooed because it is fucking pretty, the end.

As you can see, my real answer may come across as a little bit contrived. We are partly to blame that now tattoo customers are walking into regular studios and concocting backstories and reasons for their tattoo when there really isn't one.

"Oh yeah, it's a great feeling," is the answer I reply with and in doing so, I hate myself a little bit more. Conformity was never my strong point.

"So, are there any tattoos that you regret doing or is that not something you would like to share on national television?" His eyebrow cocked, looking to the audience for their approval, which he gets in the form of a laugh.

I really don't want to come across as egotistical in my answers because nothing is further than the truth. In this game, if you don't show full confidence in your abilities, then you will never get full confidence from your customers. All the way through this process, I can't help but think about the guys from the shop watching, anxiously willing me not to fuck up and make them or the industry look dumb. I think about the haters, anxiously willing me to fuck up and make myself look dumb. I often wonder if my subconscious is actually more active than my conscious. I try to keep them separate but every now and then they cross over and words leave my mouth before I can retract them in time. I take a deep breath, separate the thoughts and reply.

"I am my own worst critic, so with almost every tattoo I do, I feel I could have done better. But as I said, that is the way all artists should feel about their work. As for regrets, I don't have any specific regrets. If I feel something is not going to work as a tattoo or the person is getting it from a hate filled place, then I will simply refuse to do it. And that goes for the guys at the shop as well. It is the responsibility of every artist to make sure that the client will walk away happy with their decision but also that you, the artist, are giving them a tattoo for the right reasons in every regard. There are many shops that will just take your money and throw any old crap on there without any thought put into it on your behalf, and that's just sad. Having said all that, yes, there are tattoos that technically I would do much differently now, and I cringe when I see my older stuff, but that is a pretty universal feeling for tattoo artists across the world."

Not too bad, Megan, not too bad. The audience claps and a stupid, smug smile creeps onto my face for nailing another good point home. Get that stupid self-righteous smile off your face now!!!! Sometimes my subconscious helps me out in times like this.

"Well, Megan, I have to say you are certainly making some great points here tonight, and I for one am learning so much. It's time to take another break, folks. Make sure you come back and join us to hear the rest of Megan Banks' fascinating story of her rise to fame." Music cues, lights up.

"This is going great. You are the perfect guest, Megan. Normally I have to pry the answers out with a crowbar, but you have no problem taking the reins and running with it." I blush at his kind words and nervously laugh in acknowledgement.

"I'm so sorry for rambling on; just give me a kick when you want me to shut up." Our exchange is interrupted by Michael's makeup artist making a fuss over him again. I take the opportunity to stand up and stretch my legs. It feels good as the blood rushes down through them. My back is soaked with sweat; as it cools in the air conditioning, it sends shivers through my body. *Perfect conditions for catching a cold, young lady.* Paul waddles towards me. "Great job, sweetie, great job. You are doing perfect. Now, don't forget to plug the new season. Social media has gone nuts. We have to capitalize on this to maximum effect." I don't think Paul ever knew how to switch off his business brain; for as long as I have known him, he reverts everything back to business and making money. For example, you could be sipping your take away coffee and he will comment on how the businesses are missing a beat by not putting paid advertisements on every cup. Always thinking, always planning. This, of course, is the trait you want in your manager, but sometimes I just want to tell him to relax, chill out, it's just a cup of coffee.

"Thanks, I have no idea what I am saying. It is all one big blur, so hopefully I didn't say anything stupid." Rebecca appears with a cold glass of water and hands it to me without even asking. There are no words spoken as she is clearly listening to a voice on her oversized headset. She then scurries away like a worker ant on a mission.

"Now don't freak out, sweetie, but they just informed me five minutes ago that they will be reading out some of the Tweets people are posting as well as taking a few phone in viewers." I look at him, skeptical that this was new information to him. He knew I would freak out if he had told me before the show, but I suppose at least this way I didn't have too much time to dwell on it. "Uggggg," is the only response I can muster back to him as I head towards my seat.

"You will kill it, girl" he says, protecting his investment with as much reassurance he can muster in his voice. As I once again take the (literal) hot seat, Tristan appears with his John Wayne makeup utility belt hanging by his side.

"Hey girl, O.M.G," (he actually says the letters, not the words, Oh-My-God), "my Twittersphere has literally exploded. Yes, I know I am being a total whore by dropping your name, but if I have to live vicariously through you to gain the number of followers I just got, then that title is fine by me." He talks excitedly as he primes, plumps and dabs my makeup. A shout comes from the producer that we are back in sixty seconds. "Thanks honey," I say as he packs his brushes up and has to run off. He air blows me back a kiss. Michael returns to his seat looking refreshed and primed. I inhale as deep as I can through my nostrils and then exhale, trying to push out the anxiousness from the pits of my stomach. Like a boxer, I enter into round 3... ding, ding.

CHAPTER FIVE

"Welcome back, I am here with world famous tattoo artist, Megan Banks, star of the hit TV show *Rebel Ink*." The audience claps as if this is new information to them. "We are learning all about Megan's journey from the beginning, and it has been truly fascinating. As I mentioned before, our social media has been inundated with thousands of comments from you guys at home and we'll be reading some of them out at the end of the show. Remember to hashtag 'The Megan Banks Story'. Also, we will be taking some LIVE phone calls, so if you have any questions for Megan, you can call the number on your screen below right now. Now, back to business, Megan, they love you out there, they really do." (Cringe, cringe, cringe.)

"Aww, well I am very flattered. I don't take compliments very well, but thank you very much."
I feel the burden of sitting on this chair that so many great asses have filled – world leaders, politicians, actual famous people!!! And now, here sits my skinny ass. A nobody, in the grand scheme of things.

"Well, you should take them well, because they are well deserved." (Michael really is a sweet Man.) "So, things are going good for you now at the shop. You are making a name for yourself with your tattoos. How did the whole TV show come about?" He dives straight back into it. I feel he is under pressure for time and wants to get right to the 'good part'. I find irony in the fact that sometimes on the streets I could go days, even weeks without having a proper conversation with anybody, and now you can't shut me the hell up!

"Yeah, so my skills as a tattoo artist were getting better by the week and suddenly I was finding myself booked up fully for, like, six months ahead at a time, which was crazy because I was only tattooing about two years at that stage. The shop just kept getting busier and busier each month. The guys were all getting booked up a full year ahead, so it meant there was a lot of disappointed customers being turned away. Frankie Boy, our piercer, was also in huge demand. Sometimes I would go a full day without seeing him because he would be trapped in his studio adorning customers with shiny things."

"Oh yes, piercing has become so popular now these days, hasn't it?" Michael pounces on that one as if it was on his checklist of things to ask.

"It really has, but again there are so many bad piercers using cheap jewelery out there, you have to be very careful who you are going to. I mean, Frankie only uses implant grade 23 titanium jewelery for all his piercing work, which should be the same for every piercer, but unfortunately, just like tattooing, people go the cheap route. Cheap jewelery made of nickel can cause major infections and complications during the healing process."

Michael looks genuinely surprised, "Again, I am learning here, and also getting more concerned. My eldest daughter got her belly button pierced a few months back but only told me about it after it was done –

teenagers, right? It's pretty scary that there are people out there willing to put people at risk just to save a few bucks."

"Well, I'm sorry I don't mean to freak you out, Michael. I'm sure your daughter's piercing will be just fine, but, yes, unfortunately there are con artists out there that are not trained or educated in what they are doing. Just like tattoos, you may pay a few extra bucks, but when it comes to your body, there is no cheap option. I mean, Frankie has gone through rigorous training and has all his certificates proudly displayed on the studio wall. That's what you want to see when you walk into any shop to get a piercing done.

"Good advice," Michael says in deep thought. Sorry, Michael, I am rambling again. Back to the goddamn point, Megan.

"So anyway, Lou soon realizes we need to expand to meet the demand. Lou is one of those people gifted with a business brain and is always a few steps ahead of the game. One day, he announces we are going to have a staff meeting after work. This took us all by surprise because it was the first meeting of its kind ever called in the history of Rebel Ink. I remember Zane fretting all day thinking it was bad news and we might be shutting down, but it was the opposite. Lou laid out all the options for expansion and amongst the ideas was a wild card option of opening a shop in New York City. This option was met with a few sarcastic chuckles and 'Yeah, right' comments, but as usual Lou was already concocting a plan to make it happen. I think the whole point of the meeting was to make sure he had our support in whatever the next step was for the shop.

"Of course Boston was your hometown and you had a busy shop with a tight knit family. New York must have seemed a bizarre option to venture into?" Be careful not to offend either state here, Megan.

"Yes, at first it did, but as Lou is the daddy of the shop, he knows what is best for his kids, so sometimes we just have to shut up and listen. I mean logistically I just didn't know how he was going to do it as he was already so busy at the shop, but I will tell you something, when that man gets an idea in his head, there is just no stopping him. He has been in the game a long time, so he has loads of well-connected contacts in New York and that certainly helped him out. Little did we know that he was already in talks with TV companies about getting the show started once our new premises was ready."

"Really? So he knew there might be a chance of the show happening at this stage but didn't tell you guys?" Immediately, I feel defensive.

"Well yes, but he didn't want to worry us about it until he had something substantial to bring to the table. It was all up in the air." My words come out blunt for the first time during the interview. *Stupid thing to say, Megan.* Last thing I want to do is make Lou look bad. Michael senses my tone and tries to make amends.

"Well, that makes sense. No point getting your hopes up if there was a doubt of it not happening. So, the shop in New York came first and then the show followed?"

"The shop was always the main focus; the TV show was just an added bonus. I know a lot of people within the industry talk crap about it, but from Lou's perspective it was all about highlighting how far the industry has come and showcasing what was possible to get from your tattoo artist these days." *Okay Megan, you have made your point; now lose the defensive tone.* "So Lou pressed on, and after a year of hard work the shop was finally opened in SoHo on the lower east side. The area's rich history of art was definitely a factor in deciding to open there for Lou."

SoHo is vibrant and alive. Impeccably preserved cast iron fire escapes adorn the statement building blocks, each containing its own rich history of those who have occupied them. Cobblestone streets remain, giving it that chilled out European vibe. Restaurants are quirky and varied. Art galleries of every genre are speckled in between coffee shops and outlets. It feels cultured and yet not pompous. It is a place that I feel free.

"So, the shop in Boston stayed open? How did you manage to alternate between the two shops or did you move here straight away?"

"It was a bit of a tricky situation because we were all so booked up at the shop in Boston, so at the beginning we would each do a week in New York and then back to Boston for two weeks and vice versa. Lou assembled a strong team of artists for the New York shop, so that took the pressure off while we sorted our appointments. And then came the show. So Lou summoned us all to New York one Sunday; again we had no idea what it was about. He dropped the bombshell on us that after a year of back and forth with the TV network, he had finally secured us a deal for a ten episode season. We actually thought he was joking at first but quickly realized he was dead serious. He made it very clear that we were under no obligation to do it but did explain to us why he wanted us to do it. I have to admit I think I was in shock for a couple of days afterwards, but I had already said I was onboard for whatever was best for the shop. Actually, we all signed on pretty fast except for Sammy, who was a pretty shy guy at heart. But, after some long discussions, he decided to join his family in their new adventure and I'm so glad he did."

There were many long late night deliberations about his decision, but I like to think I convinced him to do it in the end and I am glad I did, because he truly loved his time on the show.

"I can imagine it was a surreal position for you all to suddenly be in. Did you have much time before the filming actually began?"

"No, not really. Once we were all signed up, the filming was scheduled to begin 6 weeks later. We had to find replacement artists for the shop in Boston and make the move full time to New York as the filming schedule was going to be hectic. It was a whirlwind for those six weeks to get everything figured out, but we were all very excited to get started." (Also stressed, nauseous, anxious, apprehensive, and tense.)

"So, when the filming began, how did you feel about the cameras being there? Did it take you some time to get used to it?"

"Yeah, I mean we all felt very aware of their presence at first, but honestly after a week or so, you do actually forget they are there and just get on with it. The hardest part for me was just tryna act normal (emphasis on the 'act' part). As you know, when there is a camera pointed at you, this is a very hard thing to do." Michael nods in agreement. "The other strange part was only getting to meet the customer on the day, whereas before I would have had consultations and time to design and draw a lot more, so the pressure was definitely real, as you can probably tell from my face on the show. Of course, Zane was in his element with the cameras around." I join in with the laughter from the audience. Zane is a huge hit with fans of the show.

"Obviously the time scale has been edited down to fit the show. Is that something you are aware of while you are doing a tattoo?"

"No, not really. To be honest, when it comes to actually doing the tattoo, I am just completely zoned in on that piece. As Lou always says, 'We are a tattoo shop first and a TV show second.' So, yes, you have to accommodate the camera crew to a certain point but also make sure the customer takes priority. You know, I think that's why the show works so well. There really is no bullshit from any of us. There is no script, no retakes to make stuff work better. We are a functioning shop who let the cameras roll while we work." This is partly true. There has been some things that we had to redo for some reason or another, but on the most part what you see is what you get.

"I agree, the show comes across as very genuine, when there is obviously a temptation to 'drama' things up, like what you see with a lot of other reality TV shows." Thank you, Michael, for bringing that up; you are back on my good list.

"Oh yeah, that is something we made clear from the start. This show would not work if we were forced to 'act' out any drama for the benefit of ratings or entertainment. I mean, what's the point in a reality show when it isn't actually reality at all? Having said that, some things are edited in a certain way to make a situations seem a bit more tense than they really are. Like, if you see us having a rant or a disagreement on the show, then that is 100% real. As much as we love each other, all families quarrel, but it always blows over pretty quick and is forgotten about by the end of the day. I can gladly say after all these years we are still best friends and even hang out together outside the shop on a regular basis."

Did that sound corny, Megan? Did that sound like you are telling your captive audience what they want to hear? Please shut up brain; I am trying to concentrate.

"Well that's lovely to hear because these situations can sometimes turn sour. Now, this is a textbook host question, but what has been your best and worst experience starring in the show?" *Think brain, think. I take back the 'shut up' comment, I need you back.*

"Worst – I don't want to sound fake, but I have truthfully loved every minute of making the show with my best friends. Yes, it gets tiring and stressful, but I wouldn't change that for the world. I wouldn't use the term 'worst', but the hardest episode was the one we had to film after Sammy's death. I mean that was tough, man. We all had heavy hearts but were trying to put a brave face on it. I have to say the show's producer, Matthew Davies, did an excellent job on the tribute segment he put together of Sammy – that had me sobbing when I watched it back."

"I can only imagine how hard that must have been for you guys, but as you said earlier it's what he would have wanted." The audience claps to break the awkward tension in the air.

"So the best," I say as chirpy as possible to lift the mood, "has to be the back piece I did for 'Crazy John'." The audience are clearly fans of the show as they react with cheering and clapping. Michael clearly has no idea what I am talking about.

"Well, these guys seem to love 'Crazy John', so tell us about it."

"So, as you know, we get all kinds of customers from all walks of life into the shop, but every now and again you get a unique one like John. John basically went off grid around twenty years ago. He was actually an investment banker here in New York City but got fed up running the rat race and retreated to the Rocky Mountains. He built himself a log cabin up there and lived off the land. After almost twenty years he decided to return to New York to see if things had changed in his absence. He found they had, but not for the better, and decided he would return to his log cabin after a brief visit. He was staying with his sister here in Manhattan, and he had told her he was looking to get a tattoo before he left and she actually put him forward for the show. So, the producers gave me a quick rundown of John's story, but they didn't know what tattoo he wanted exactly. Normally, we would have some time to plan and draw something up, but this was a unique situation. I was actually dying to meet him to hear his story."

"When he arrived, he looked like the definition of Grizzly Adams. (I'm sure the irony of this does not escape him.) He was as warm and charming as you guys saw him to be on the show. I remember him jokingly saying, "My God, I have never seen a woman with so many tattoos, but come to think of it, I haven't seen a woman in almost twenty years, so I guess that doesn't count." We hit it off right away. He was very curious about how the tattoo was actually done and I showed him the machines we used and explained as best I could. He reminded me that when he left New York, tattoos were actually illegal and it was all very underground (tattoos were only re-legalized here in 1997). He was truly amazed at how far it has progressed. He showed me a tattoo he had poked into his forearm using a pine needle and burnt out ash from the fire while living in the wild. I am never one to usually be a fan of D.I.Y. tattoos, but I loved the organic nature of the little sun symbol he had done."

I continued, "So anyway, the cameras started rolling and I still didn't know what he wanted done. I certainly was not expecting to hear what he actually wanted. As he was explaining his story to the camera, he kept referring to 'his kids' living with him in the cabin. He spoke as a proud parent, 'I always made sure my kids were fed before I worried about me.' I had just presumed his 'kids' were from a previous marriage and he had taken them with him to live the life off grid. But no, as it transpired, 'his kids' were actually three black bears." Michael pantomimes an open mouth shock face.

"Yep, turns out he saved three young cubs after their mother had been killed by a hunter. He took them in and literally raised them as his children. The tattoo he wanted was a portrait of the three of them across his back, from shoulder to shoulder. This was right up my alley, but he only had a really old faded Polaroid photograph of the three of them when they were cubs that I had to work from, and I had to draw the tattoo up right there on the spot. The tattoo took eight hours to complete and he sat like a rock. The show captured some of the stories he told during the process, but he had a good eight hours' worth of material. I even told him that he should have his own show. He loved the idea of that. So yeah, that was one of the best moments, getting to meet John and hear his story. He was delighted with the finished piece and told me I captured his kids perfectly. I added in their names under each portrait, Henry, Jacob and Massey."

A perfectly timed image of the finished piece appears on the screen behind us. Either these guys were amazingly well prepared or the researcher was quick off the mark in Google searches.

"What a fascinating story, and the detail in that tattoo is phenomenal. So did John return to the Rockies?"

"Oh yeah, he went back. He told me he couldn't bear," (if I was quick enough I would have made a joke about 'bear' here), "to be away from his kids. But he promised me he would come back and visit once a year, so I look forward to seeing him again soon. He actually invited me and the guys to come and visit him up in his cabin sometime. This is something we will definitely do when we get the time. I am so curious to see how he lives and to meet his bears."

"Oh, I would love to hear how that goes, so keep us posted on that one. What a great story.
Now, tattooing is not all you are famous for, is it? You also dabble in a bit of the modelling world."

"Well, let's just be clear, I am no model, Michael. I have done a few ad campaigns, but only for stuff that I feel strongly about, like the PETA campaign I did against hunting animals for fur." The billboard image appears on the screen. Me standing in what I suppose you could call an artistic nude pose, showing as much of my tattoos as possible without showing everything else, and the slogan 'Get Inked, Not Minked' written in a bold italic font underneath. It was only when I saw the images from the photoshoot that I had realized how heavily tattooed I had gotten. When you see yourself on a regular basis, you just don't notice it, but when you see yourself out of context, it is completely different. My stomach all the way up to my chest was now almost full with intricate designs influenced by Japanese art. Dragon's heads sit on the point of each shoulder; they are my protectors. A samurai warrior consumes the right side of my ribs (that one fucking hurt). A stunning geisha sits on the other side (this one also fucking hurt). The big one, the 'job stopper' (as in a regular job that adheres to discrimination policies, depending on how you look and not your ability), the one that takes you from being 'tattooed' to being 'heavily tattooed', that is my neck piece. It is a snow owl, his body and head centered in the middle of my throat, and his sprawled wings wrap around each side of my neck, the tips reaching up as far as behind my ears. It was done by Trent over two grueling sessions, which in total took eighteen hours. It may not be everyone's cup of tea, but I love it. My legs were also filling up with various images that don't really have any cohesion to them; everything from cute girlie images to snarling skulls fill up various spaces. I hate looking at photos of myself, but Franco Willis, the photographer, did an amazing job with this one and I actually liked it.

"What a great image and a strong message that goes with it. My word, you have some amount of ink on your body," he says with a genuine tone of shock attached. "You have also been known to strut your stuff on the catwalk. Was that fun to do?"

"Again, I have done two fashion shows, but they were for charity, I am 5'5", so I don't think I can quite cut it as a supermodel, Michael. But yeah, they were great fun and for a great cause too."

"You must get recognized a lot on the streets now, Megan. How are you coping with this element of being a celebrity?"

"I still find it very strange as I am just a tattoo artist that happens to tattoo on a TV show. I'm not a celebrity in any regard. It was just the right place and right time for me, but really it could have been anyone finding themselves in my position. I suppose it has gotten more and more common as the show has gotten bigger over the last couple of years. I am quite a shy person, so the attention took me a while to get used to. Most people are cool and I try to make time for a photo with them if they want one. Some people can be a bit rude or maybe just oblivious to certain situations. Like, if I am out for lunch with my friends and in the middle of eating my pasta, they will come over and want pictures and stuff. I think it's more annoying for my friends as they are not used to dealing with it, and my freaking pasta is getting cold, dude."

I try to lighten my words so I don't come across as being an ungrateful bitch. I see my opportunity to flip it around and ask Michael a question, "You have being dealing with it a lot longer than I have. How do you find it?"

"Ah, when you are an old dog like me, Megan, you find that sort of attention dwindles down over the years. Nobody wants the wrinkly old man in photos anymore." I join the audience in their sympathetic 'awwwww', but I feel he is just being humble by saying that, and unlike me he knows not to piss off his fans by saying it's annoying sometimes.

"I'm sure that's not true. You are a national treasure and I will be wanting a selfie with you after the show," I say to assuage his feelings.

"Well, that's very nice of you to say, but, yes, to answer your question properly, it can be difficult to deal with. It's an invasion of your privacy, but it comes with the territory, I suppose."

I can't really blame him for setting up the cue to his next question, although this subject is the one thing that Paul had outlined was out of bounds to ask me about. Although it had been much publicized by the press, we had been working in conjunction with the Police Department over the last year to quash the story.

"Sometimes there are people who take it too far, and I know you have experienced that to an extreme degree." Tip-toeing around the subject like a fat lady to the fridge, on a diet but with the late night munchies. Paul was not going to be happy. "Is that something you are comfortable talking with us about?" Clever wording to pass the liability back to my corner. *Decision time again, Megan.* I am not obligated to answer, but yet I feel obligated to answer. *We have worked hard to play this down and the situation is getting better. Do you really want it to flare up again? He would surely be watching. You would be feeding into his delusional disorder.* My mouth moves before I have made up my mind.

"Yeah, it has been a difficult and complicated situation." You didn't answer 'No', giving Michael the opportunity to probe further.

"Yes, I mean we talked about invasion of privacy, but this is taking it to a whole new level. I believe you even had to move because of it?" 'IT', yet again a clever wording, as to incite me to talk about the situation without directly asking me. Well played, sir.

"Yeah, it got pretty intense and I didn't feel safe anymore. I have had to move four times since arriving in New York because of it." Short, direct answers, but you are talking about it, Megan. It feels good to talk about it. This is the most fucked up counseling session in the world.

"Awful, and is this still going on?" Is what going on, Michael? I would love to cock my eyebrow and call him on the bullshit, but I refrain. What he is asking me about is the psychopath stalker that has harassed me for the last seven years on and off. I often found myself pondering his actions whenever he went quiet. Do stalkers take holidays? Was he just too busy with work to stalk that week? Maybe he was on a family vacation? The stalking was never physical. Many disagreed, but this made it worse for me. Not being able to put a face to the torment made me feel completely powerless. He was meticulous and calculating. Never dropping his guard to allow himself to be caught. I wracked my brain trying to figure out if it was somebody I knew. I became suspicious of everyone. Could they be the one? It's the question I always asked myself obsessively after every encounter. Ironic that an obsessive stalker has in turn made me obsessive and determined to find out who was behind it.

"Yep, unfortunately stalkers don't seem to lose interest too easily." There's that ugly word 'stalker' now aired on national TV, no taking it back now. I can imagine him watching, his eyes lighting up at the mention of his 'title'. Acknowledgment – apparently that's what stalkers craved but in an anonymous form. Contradictions, commonplace amongst irrational thoughts. To acknowledge his existence will further fuel his desire for you – this is what the experts had told me.

"It must be a terrifying ordeal. I don't want to push you on this topic as I know it is uncomfortable for you speak about, so I will just say that I hope whoever it is putting you through this, if you are watching, it is time for it to stop. No good has or will come from your actions, so I appeal to your conscience to stop the harassment and the torment of this young girl. Do the right thing."

This completely takes me by surprise. Was his statement rehearsed or fed through his earpiece? The camera panned in on his face for dramatic effect. Was his tone threatening enough to spark a triggered defensive attack from my predator? This might be the ratings lottery win for the network, but this was my life being put in jeopardy. I may sound overdramatic, but so would you in my situation. Surely, Paul had followed through on our decision to prohibit them speaking about this on national television?

The newspapers had had a field day with the story when I stupidly spoke about it on the show. Things got worse pretty fast after that. The letters increased (always printed, never written). The phone calls became more frequent (even changing numbers twice a month did not deter them). My social media pages hacked and filled with obscene art (The police worked hard to try and find the owner of the art, but every lead led them to a dead end.). And the worst, the emotionally damaging and draining part of my stalker experience, the late night knocks at my apartment door. Art pieces crudely stuck to it with blue tack that contained no fingerprint evidence. Art that always contained my face in a contorted, almost unrecognizable form, but you still knew it was me. Art that freaked me out to my very core. The one image that will stay with me until my dying day, my eyes peering out from a severed goat's head placed over mine, trapped under the bloody dismembered head, just like I felt trapped by his actions. That was the first time I had felt in fear of my life. This person clearly wanted to do harm to me.

I already lived in a state of perpetual anxiety, but it had been getting better. Now the thoughts of returning to the dread because of a few flippant words (no matter how pure the intentions may have been) on a television show deeply worried me. I really don't think I could cope with living like that again. Karma had come around 360. Irony seems to follow my life like a plague. I actually felt safer on the streets than I did in an apartment with locked doors. As the audience's claps subside, I feel nauseas and tense. I feel powerless.

CHAPTER SIX

"We are almost coming to the end of the show, folks, and I think you will all agree it has been fascinating listening to Megan's story. We could talk all night, we really could. But now it is time to hand the reigns over to you guys at home. We have some callers and some video callers lined up to ask a few questions of their own. The response on Twitter has broken all of our previous records for the show, so we thank every one of you for getting in touch. We have our first caller on the line, Michelle from Florida. Welcome to the show; what would you like to ask Megan?"

I was still rattled from the 'stalker' topic being forced upon me, catching me totally off guard as I was sure this topic was off limits. I was anxious, but I think I was born anxious. As far back as I can remember, it was always there, churning my stomach like a cake mill. My mind would always take me to the worst case scenario, and then play it out to its full abrupt conclusion. A worrier is how my teachers described me as a child, among the clichéd evaluations that I was also a 'dreamer' and 'easily distracted'. I suppose they were all true observations that carried with me through my life, but still, pretty harsh to judge on a seven-year-old. The high pitched tone of Michelle's nervous voice comes over the P.A. system and snaps me out of my anxiety coma.

"Oh, hi Michael and hi Megan. Can I just say I am a huge fan of both you guys?"

"Well, that's very nice of you to say. I'm glad Megan hasn't stolen all of my thunder tonight."

I chime in with, "Hey Michelle, thank you." It is all I can muster up in this strange three-way phone call. Now ask your question and don't make this awkward.

"My question for Megan is just some advice on breaking into the industry. I am currently in my first year of a fine art degree, but I really want to become a tattoo artist. You are like my role model, and I hope I can be as talented as you someday."

Ah, Jesus, Michelle, you are sweet to say, but now I have to acknowledge your compliment and reply with my mouth full of humble pie; pie mouth does not look good on TV.

"Well, you are making me blush here, but I am glad I inspire you. You are definitely on the right track being in college studying art. As I said earlier, that is the foundation of any good tattoo artist. I was lucky in the sense that Lou happened across me that day, but it never usually works like that. Pick the best shop with the best artists and show them how badly you want it. First of all, having a really strong portfolio to show them your drawing ability is the best way to get their attention. Draw all styles, but make sure you can draw with an understanding of tattoo designs too. Getting tattooed off the artists at the shop can build a good foundation, and during your session you can get to ask some questions. Offer to come in and clean the shop and help out in your spare time. This way you will gain their trust and respect. The worst thing people do when looking for an apprenticeship is to ask over an email or Facebook. This is just lazy and flippant, and you will rarely get any reply from a busy shop. An artist wants to speak with you face to face to see how serious you are about it. Don't be afraid if the answer is no. I have so many people come through the shop, they ask once and then I never see them again. It can be a scary thing going into a shop and showing credible artists your own drawings for them to judge you. If your work is not up to the standard required, then most decent artists will offer advice and guidance of what you need to work on. So, if you get that advice, work on it and then come back and show them that you are making an effort. This doesn't always guarantee an apprenticeship because you may not be the right fit or the shop just isn't taking anybody on. But you have to try, and then if a position becomes available at the shop, you will be the first number they will call because you have showed them the desire you have. Unfortunately, it is a bit tougher for us girls. Yes, the industry is drastically changing and there are more and more female artists breaking through, but it is still a male dominated industry, so be prepared to work that extra bit harder to gain their respect. And lastly, you cannot be too sensitive in your nature, as it can be a boisterous environment to work in at the best of times, but don't take any of their crap either."

Michael joins in on the applause, "Well Michelle, you aren't going to get any better advice than that." The phone line stays silent. Did she loose signal? Had she even heard my empowering wisdom bestowed upon her? C'mon girl, I'm not going to repeat it – speak! Finally, the line crackles, just as the producer is going to move it on.

"Oh my gosh, that is amazing advice. Thank you so much!"

"You are very welcome and hopefully I will see you tattooing some day in the future." I do genuinely mean that. I want to see more female artists giving the men a run for their money. In the tattoo industry, it can be a chauvinistic world, but I can be a chauvinistic girl.

"Thanks Michelle, okay now we have Samantha from Manhattan on the line. Welcome Samantha, what's your question for Megan?"

"Hi, I actually have two questions, if that's alright? First, if I want to get a tattoo off you. Can I come down to Rebel Ink even if I'm not on the show?" Ah c'mon Samantha, this question could have been answered by a quick trip to my website.

"Hey Samantha. Yeah, I mean the shop is a fully functioning studio even when the show is not being filmed. I divide my time between there and the shop back in Boston, and I also work the tattoo convention circuit around the world as much as possible. So, excluding when we are filming, I have a waiting list of over a year, which is crazy but if you are willing to wait, by all means you can book in with me."

"I'm sure you must get a lot of fans of the show just coming to the shop to meet you guys and not necessarily to get a tattoo done?" Michael asks from a perspective of being on the inside for so many years.

"Oh yeah, we really get loads, so in that regard the major difference with the New York shop is having security at the doors all year round. This is for our protection but also for our customers' best interest. They are paying for a service and the artist can't be distracted by people asking for pictures and autographs every two minutes. We all try our best to accommodate for the fans once our work is done. It can get a bit crazy down there, so I like to get back to Rebel Ink in Boston when I can for a more relaxed environment."

"I can imagine it getting a bit crazy when you are trying to concentrate on your work alright, so Samantha what's your second question?"

"Thank you for that, Megan. I will be booking in with you as soon as possible. My second question is about Billy. Are you guys still dating and is it tough with both of your hectic lives?"

Cheeky question Samantha.

So, I suppose I should explain who Billy is. By Billy, she means Billy Bane, guitar player for rock n' roll band PROPANE. We met two years back at a charity auction event and hit it off immediately. To describe his look is to describe every typical rock star prototype in the book. You know the look, long rough cut hair dyed jet black, his locks hugging his chiseled cheek bones, milky white skin that made his green eyes pop, his image confident enough to adorn 'guy liner', skinny black jeans with chains that hang down by his side and sleeveless denim jackets with band patches stitched in crudely. Yeah, he was a rock star by the numbers, but my god, he carried it well. So, I ended up tattooing him just before he set off on tour to Australia. I was like a giddy school girl that day, totally out of character for me, so I knew that there was something special about him. He entrusted me to recreate his band's latest album cover called *Take the Reins*. The artist, Robbie Birkshaw, had drawn this amazing four horse drawn chariot with the grim reaper steering them to impending doom (my interpretation, don't quote me on that). He was already pretty full up with ink, but we found a sweet spot on his top left shoulder to place it. I felt enormous pressure as I knew that the artist, Robbie, would be studying in detail how close I got to recreating his work. We talked and joked the whole way through, obvious flirting, boy meets girl, girl meets boy kind of stuff.

By the end of it he was stoked about his tattoo, and I have to admit I was too. It had turned out perfect. And then, just as I walked him to the door, he asked me out. I said yes and a year's worth of a relationship ensued. Because of our profiles, once word got out it was covered quite heavily from the press, and that made it hard. But harder still was our time schedules and trying to make it work. His band was getting bigger and my life was getting busier. My stalker issue freaked him out and he hated coming over to my place. I think he felt powerless to help, which goes against the macho protective gene most men have, so it added to the pressure of the relationship.

"No, I am afraid we aren't a couple anymore, but we remain really good friends. Billy is the sweetest guy, but our lives are just so busy we couldn't find the time to make it work." It still hurt. Thanks for bringing it up, Samantha. The only man in my life now is my cat, Jake.

"Aww, I'm sorry to hear that. You guys made such a great couple." And how would you know we made a great couple, stranger on the phone? *Now, now, don't be bitter, Megan, just because you couldn't make it work with the one guy who you loved and who loved you back. No need to take it out on her.* Michael speaks before I have time to thank her for the kind words.

"Okay, thank you, Samantha. Now we have a video link lined up here and Megan you might recognize a few familiar faces." The screen lights up behind us and to my total surprise it is Zane, Trent, Mike and Frankie staring back at me. I clasp my hand over my mouth and burst into a fit of laughter. For no particular reason at all Zane is wearing a novelty 'Jolly Roger' pirate hat. I immediately wished I was there; hanging out with those guys was always so much fun and was sure to end in mischievous adventures.

"Hey Megan," they all shout over each other at once.

"Hi guys, well this is awkward."

Michael tries to join in on the bravado. "Looks like you are having a fun party there, fellas." "Well, we kind of have to seeing as we weren't asked to be on the show," Trent says in his usual sarcastic deadpan tone that not everyone gets unless you know him well. I quickly retort to affirm that he is in fact joking, "Sorry, Michael doesn't let riff raff on his show, Trent." Laughter all round.

Zane, lovely as always, says, "We are so proud of you. You should so run for president, girl." "Aww, thanks sweetie, wish I was there with you guys." 'There' was Frankie's apartment; I could tell by the artwork hanging on the walls.

And then it happened, the clear loser of the dare. The impending act that was making them so hyper and giggly. On national live television, representing the tattoo artists of the world. A giant, bare, hairy ass gets pressed up against the screen in all of its squidgy glory. The audience, myself included, tilt our heads and squint hard to make out what it actually is for a moment. But as the owner of the bottom slightly pulls back from the camera, it becomes very clear that, yes, that is in fact a grown man's ass cheeks being displayed for the world to see. Before the owner gets revealed, the camera feed gets cut, the screaming laughs of the observers on their side lingering in our ears. My hand returns to my mouth with an open gasp.

Ink Princess

The audience pauses to take in what they have just witnessed and then erupt into roars of laughter, soon joined by myself and Michael. Tears fill my eyes as the more I think about it, the harder the laughs come. Michael sinks his head into folded arms, unable to compose himself. I can see the shoulders of cameramen shaking up and down as they cannot help the flow of laughter taking over their bodies. The most juvenile of all humor can unite the world in laughter. There is no politics or language barriers, just a great big bare ass, mooning a camera live on TV. Brilliant. A good solid minute of this goes by before it begins to simmer down.

Michael, wiping the tears from his eyes and clearing his throat, turns to me and says, "I have been doing this job for a long time and I really thought I had seen it all, but never, ever have I seen anything like that." In a strange way, I feel so proud of my guys. I can just imagine them rolling around on the floor in disbelief that he actually went through with it. Who's ass was it? I don't know for sure, but I am going to have to guess it was Zane, because that guy is hairy!

"I can only apologize to you guys for having to witness that, especially to anybody eating their dinner at home. Don't worry, I will have a word with them boys," I say in my mother tone. I am of course joking. I am well used to their pranks and messing around. I will call them later and find out who the 'ass bandit' was, and we will laugh about it once more.

"Well, I hope you do, Megan. I mean, there is just no editing that on live television." With that, Michael's laughs re-emerge from his belly and he begins chuckling away again. Finally, he gets it together enough to speak, "Okay folks, this is our last caller of the night, and I for one am glad it is not a video call after what we have just witnessed. We have John on the line calling from your hometown of Boston. Hello John, welcome to the show. What would you like to ask Megan?" Silence. Deathly silence. Our ears pricked waiting for a tone to emerge. Nothing. "Hi John, are you with us?" My toes curl up tight with the awkwardness. Finally, a voice. Cool, calm and collected, unlike the previous callers tonight.

"I have followed you from the very beginning. I have watched you grow into the fine woman you have become. I know you better than any of them, Megan." He speaks with clarity and accent free. Yes, he was American but with no distinctive accent that you could place. Silence. I feel a familiar chill run down my body. I shift uneasily in my seat. Michael looks a little confused. "Very good John, and what is your question for Megan?" Silence. Deathly silence.

"It is not my place to ask the questions; I invite Megan to ask me a question. You have so many who try to speak for you, but no one actually listens. I listen, Megan. I will always listen." Michael's look of concern matches mine. That feeling of dread comes back to visit me. I couldn't be hearing the voice behind the years of silent abuse. This has to be a wannabe, a hoaxer looking for attention in the most fucked up way possible. Sweat again, but this time it runs cold down my boiling face. Like a rabbit caught in the headlights, I was frozen stiff – fear, the most powerful emotion that can grip the human body in an instant, rendering it useless in defense. Endorphins and adrenaline combining to fix you to a chemical coma. Michael didn't speak this time. He just looked at me with, 'Well, do you want to ask this guy anything or will we just shut it down?' I wanted to cry, I wanted to scream, but nothing came out.

Finally, my voice reaches the tip of my mouth and my words come out sounding foreign. "Do-I-know-you?" This was the burning question I had for all of these years, so if this was the guy, if this was my one question, then I am glad it is this one. Silence. Calculating. Evaluating.

"Of course you know me. I am the one who has kept you safe for all of these years. I don't need vindication like all the others crave from you, Megan, I know you love me and I love you too. Someday I will show you that you are not alone. I will prove you can trust me and I will protect you. Forever."

As the information resonates in my mind, Michael is now on the defensive. Escalation of the situation could further be fueled with what he says next. I want it to stop; I want it to all go away. This is living out my worst nightmare.

"Now you listen here, John, or whatever your real name is, this phone call is being tracked and we will be contacting the NYPD. You are clearly disturbed and need help. Now, we can get you that help, but you have to turn yourself in. You are not helping this girl. You are terrifying her. This has to stop, John. You need help."

I wish this was one of my paranoid delusions, but this was real. This was happening on live television. Seven years of being tormented in my own skin. So many emotions run through my brain all at once, the strangest one being a sense of relief. Relief of finally hearing a voice. After years begging for a voice on the countless silent phone calls. In the height of my paranoia and anxiety, I had convinced myself that I was going insane and all of the events were an accumulation of my overactive imagination. Here was confirmation that what I had experienced was in fact real. I find solace in this as a strange and twisted consolation against all of the other emotions bubbling to the surface. I wouldn't blame viewers for being skeptical, an act played out for shock tactics. But not even an Oscar nominee could act out the genuine terror etched across my face. We wait in anticipation to hear the voice again, but our expectancy is dispersed with the single beep of a dial tone. He has hung up. Relief and frustration – I'm glad the voice has gone, but I am left with so many burning questions that remain perched on the tip of my tongue.

Michael's eyes are fixed on me; he looks genuinely concerned. My head stays down, but my eyes dart from side to side uncontrollably. I want the ground to open up and offer me a slide that will gently transport me to the sanctity of my bed. My fantasy is disrupted by Michael's voice. His words come out soft and slow.

"Megan, I can't imagine how hard that must have been for you, but I think everyone will agree you handled it remarkably well." He glances to the audience to coax them into a round of applause, which they do. I know he is trying to help, but I can't help but feel anger now, as my brain realizes it was his flippant questions that brought up the topic I had explicitly requested not to be asked about. Strangers slapping their hands together is not going to make this situation any better, and once they file out of studio 5A, it will be my life that carries the burden of tonight's events.

"Now, Megan, I am being told that the phone line is being traced as we speak, but let's not rule out the chance of an imposter. Maybe this creep heard you discussing the stalker that has plagued your life and decided to take advantage and play a cruel joke. If this is the case, I implore you to give yourself up and contact us here at the station."

I can hardly believe the bullshit being spoken. An imposter? This was not an imposter; I knew that now. I could almost smell his musky scent as he spoke. The scent that lingered in my apartment block hallway, the scent I so often smelled in my car park, a smell that scared me to my core. I knew this smell was him. How I knew, I really don't know, but it made my skin come alive with fear. Just hearing that voice triggered my nasal gland memories into overdrive and I hated it.

"Are you okay?" Michael asks with empathy, but I also detect a suppressed sense of glee of how good this situation is for live television and their ratings. I know I have a tendency for paranoia, but in this situation I think that I am justified.

"I'm a bit freaked out, to be honest, but I don't really want to talk anymore about it, please." I just wanted to get this interview over with so I could speak with the police and see if they could trace the call. I give Michael a look to confirm that if he pushed me on this there was going to be trouble. Wisely, he takes heed of my death stare and he moves on. Clearly, he is off course from his interview strategy and for the first time tonight he is visibly flustered.

"So, eh, Megan, what's next for you?"

Oh, you know, probably impending doom from a crazed stalker that you instigated to come on national TV and reveal himself to me after seven years. Of course, I didn't say this, but I hoped that in some way he knew that's what I was thinking. I composed myself once more.

"Well, we have just finished filming the new season of *Rebel Ink*, so that will air sometime in the fall. I can't wait for people to see this one. There has been so much happening since you last saw us and I really feel this is the best season yet." My words come out with a quiver attached. There you go, Paul, the plug I had promised you has been delivered. Michael seems to have settled down a bit, but he still squirms anxiously on his chair.

"I'm sure your fans are all dying to see it. You also have a clothing label. Can you tell us a little about that?"

Oh my God, he's actually going to murder me. Will I have to move again? Will I have to hire 24-hour security? Back to insomnia, back to sleeping with the lights on, back to leaving on the TV so that I don't imagine noises late at night. Fuck you, Michael. I have to quench my inner dialogue before I speak.

"Yeah, so it's something I have been working on for a while now. It's basically an art collective of designs done by some of my favorite tattoo artists that I hand select. They custom design a piece and then we run a limited number of shirts and hoodies. Each one of the guys at the shop has done some awesome designs, and they are busy working on some new ones for next season. I named the label 'Art Junkie'. I thought it represented the artists involved quite well as each one is addicted to their craft in some shape or form."

"And have you done some designs for it as well, Megan?"

"To be honest, I felt really self-conscious after I started the label and all of these amazing artists were producing the most incredible designs to give me. There was no way I could match their skill. But, finally after months of working on it, I decided to run one of my designs about three months back. I'm glad I did, but I think I will leave the rest up to my friends. The pressure was massive and I don't really want to go through it again."

I notice my tone has changed. Gone is the nervous, chirpy, fast-paced chatter and it is now replaced with a somber, methodical one. I am mentally drained and quite sure I can't take much more of this. A breakdown on national TV is the last thing I wanted, but I can feel the tears welling up from behind my eyes, aching to get out and release the tomb of tension soaring through my body. Years on the streets had taught me to hide my emotions, as to display them out there could easily get you killed. Like vultures prey on the weak, you let your guard down and you end up being the victim. Thankfully, Michael's next words are impeccably timed against my predicament of tears.

"Well, folks, we are almost out of time. I'm sure you will all agree it has been a fascinating show learning of Megan's rise to the top. I have personally learned so much tonight and I thank Megan for her patience with an old dinosaur like myself not having a clue about her world in tattooing. You have definitely made me think differently about it, as I am sure you have for many of our viewers tonight. You should be very proud of what you have achieved and I wish you all of the continued success in the world."

As the audience's claps resume, I let a single tear spill out but disguise it with a fake cough and quickly wipe it away. His words seem genuine and not fed from his earpiece; this added even more fuel to my already bubbling concoction of emotions. As the claps subside, I choose my words carefully. "Thank you for the kind words. I am glad I got to share my story with you tonight. This is the first time I have spoken publicly about the events that have lead me to where I am today and, to be honest, I wasn't even sure I was going to share that part of my life until the words came flowing out. The main reason I don't really talk about it is for the same reason I never begged for money on the streets. I don't want to see that look of sympathy or pity in anyone's eyes. The events that happened in my life made me a survivor. You don't depend on anyone to look after you; you learn to look after yourself. I know how lucky I was to get out of that situation and I have Lady Miriam and Lou to thank for that. Yes, there were many times I just wanted to just give up, but this life is not predetermined and you really never know what is around the corner. As bad as things get, there is always hope. I love my life; getting paid to do the one thing that I love most in this world is literally my dream come true. I really don't know where I would be now if things had of worked out differently, but no matter what I would have continued my path as an artist in some shape or form – that is just in my blood. No matter what this world throws at me, I'm going to throw it right back. So, if one deluded creep thinks he is going to ruin what I have worked my ass off to create, then they will feel the wrath of all my being and be sorry they ever crossed my path." I take a breath.

What have I just done? I will tell you what – I have let my emotions override my brain. I have made a speech led by emotion and not rational thought. I have just challenged my stalker to come and get me. I may have just sealed my fate. The audience rise from their seats to

Ink Princess

give a standing ovation, which makes me cringe once again in embarrassment. Michael has to wait patiently for the noise to die down before he can speak.

"Very well said, Megan. You really are a fine role model to a generation. And hey, you may even see me in the shop for my tattoo someday soon – stranger things have happened." I try to break a smile through my trembling lip.

"That would be awesome," is the only response I can muster up.

"Okay, just before we end the show, I would just like to read out some of your Tweets you have been posting, and wow, there are literally thousands of them. Thank you all for getting in touch. Sorry guys, I just need my glasses for this bit. I did tell you all that I am getting old. Right, so here are just a few we have picked out:

'Huge *Rebel Ink* fan, can't wait for the new season #MeganRocks'

'Megan is best tattoo artist in the world. Hopefully I can get some ink off her someday'

'What a story, I had no idea how hard she had it, much respect #girlpower'

'Who thinks there needs to be a part 2 to this interview? #bringherback'"

"I could literally go on all night with these, Megan. You have made a huge connection with these people tonight. What about that last one? You think you would come back on for us sometime, and we can see how it's all going for you?" I'm not stupid; clearly that Tweet was chosen as a gateway to ask me back to get all the juicy details about how my psycho story plays out. That's if I am still alive to tell that story.

C'mon, Megan, this is your chance to stand up to the powers of the TV network, call them on their bullshit, tell them your life is more important than their ratings. What was that big, powerful rant you had a few minutes ago about being a strong, independent woman? We can do this. Now speak.

"Oh, sure Michael, I would love to."

Really? That's you sticking it to them? You really are pathetic. I am ashamed to be the voice inside your head right now. I think it's time for me to pack up and leave. Let's see how long you last without me.

"Great, I truly look forward to it. I will be tuning in to the new series with my girls at home. They will think I am so cool for that I'm sure. Once more, thank you to the wonderful Megan Banks. Goodnight and take care folks. See you next time."

The music starts up and the lights dim down. It feels good to get a break from the burning illumination of the high powered spotlights on my face. Michael rises from his seat and awkwardly makes his way over to me. He extends his hand for what I think is a handshake, but he then places it gently on my shoulder.

"Megan, that was just amazing. In all of my years I have never had anything come close to that interview. I am just sorry it was ruined by that caller getting through. I know how scared and angry you must be, but I assure you I will put the measures in place to make sure that you are safe and this guy is tracked down. My girls idolize you, and if they turn out to be anything like the wonderful young woman you are, then I would be a proud father." His words are sweet, but why does that hand on my shoulder feel like he is commiserating me, like someone has just died?

"Thank you, it was all going so well up until that point. You really made it easy for me to speak about those things I would never normally talk about." I decide there really is no point in getting angry with him. I know he is there to do a job and it is the director in his earpiece that controls what he asks. At this point I really want to speak with Paul, and I just hope he didn't betray my wishes or it could be the end of our relationship. Our moment is interrupted by runners waiting to take our microphones off. The distraction is a welcome relief. As my microphone is being untangled, I spot the usual smiling Tristan with a concerned look on his face approaching me.

"Oh my God, honey, are you okay? That was so freaking intense." His bulging eyes full of worry.

"Yeah, I'm alright, I just want it to all be over now." I am distracted by the audience shuffling out of the building, speaking in hushed tones, clearly evaluating what has just happened before their eyes.

"Listen, you did great, honey. I wouldn't have handled that situation like you just did. I don't know if anybody has told you, but the cops are here and they want to speak with you when you are ready."

The news of cops being here is both reassuring and terrifying. The presence of them confirms a real threat; my life as I know it is about to change forever. My eyes scan the floor for Paul, but he is nowhere to be seen. If the voice in my head hadn't just vacated me, it would be screaming, *He's guilty, definitely guilty, why else would he not be straight over to you to defend himself against allegations of betraying your trust?*

Had the voice really left me or was it just trying to trick me into thinking it had? Jesus, Megan, maybe a mental institution is the safest place for you. I run my conflicting inner dialogue while people speak around me, oblivious to my crazy thoughts. Then, lurking in the shadows, I make out the robust figure of Paul. He is waving his arms around like a lunatic.

Politely, I apologize to Tristan to excuse me and I make a beeline in Paul's direction. As I get Closer, I can see his face is bright purple and his words are coming out with venom. He is clearly pissed. As he takes a breath, he notices me walking towards him and his tensed up shoulders drop down. He exhales heavily and places his chubby fingers on the sweat drenched bridge of his nose.

"Listen, Megan, I am getting this mess sorted out. Don't you worry bout a thing." For as long as Paul has been in my life, he has always been very protective of me. He has lived through the turmoil of my stalker situation first hand and has seen me at my lowest point. Was I wrong to suspect him? I don't think suspicion is wrong; suspicion is human nature and it can keep you protected from people willing to take advantage. I have to know either way. I want to ask him direct to his face.

"Paul, why the hell did they ask me about the stalker situation when we agreed that was off the table to discuss? I mean, we agreed on that, right?" I study his face; he looks hurt.

"Listen, honey, you have known me a long time, right? After everything we have been through, do you really think I wouldn't follow through on your request? Do you think I would put your life in jeopardy to give these monkeys some added drama? I distinctly told them that topic was off the table, but they decided to go ahead and ignore me. So now I am going to find whoever is responsible and then we are going to sue their ass." I have never seen Paul so animated before, his rushing blood making him look even more constricted by his tight suit. I am relieved to hear his words, and would much rather him be on my side during this whole situation.

"I know, Paul. I'm sorry, but I just had to ask. My mind is a mess right now." His phone has been ringing the whole time. He finally reaches into his pocket to retrieve it. "Sorry, honey, I have to take this." As soon as he answers, he flies straight back into his rant into the poor ear of the receiver on the other end. I felt proud of how serious he was taking this and this confirmed he had my best interest at heart. As I turn to find the solace of my dressing room, I literally bump into the ever scurrying Rebecca. This frightens me more than it normally would as my wits are on the very edge. Unapologetic, and her voice monotone, as if she was reading off a shopping list she said, "The police want to speak with you. They are waiting for you in your dressing room, so I'm here to take you back down there now." At least I can't accuse her of taking pity on me. I don't think much would phase Rebecca.

As I follow her back down the winding corridors, I keep my eyes peered beyond her figure to make sure there is no one waiting to grab me. My paranoia is in full flight – shouldn't there be security with us? I kick myself as this afterthought reaches me. it's your own fault for not insisting on it, Megan. Silly girl. As we turn the last corner, I stop dead in my tracks, my feet frozen to the floor. A tall, scruffy man in a long black trench coat that almost reaches the floor is standing there. His hands buried in his pockets, he stares as Rebecca gets closer. My heart is beating through my mouth; my breathing becomes short and fast. Before I can hold it back, I scream at the top of my lungs, "Rebecca, stop!!!" My scream echoes and bounces off the walls of the long corridor. I am powerless to help. Forget about fight or flight; I could do neither. This is it. He has me now; this is how it all ends.

Diary Entry:

My psychiatrist has convinced me that these diary entries will help me deal with the turmoil that I faced in my younger years. I had always kept diaries from around the age of ten as a way of telling all of my problems without having to confide in anyone. Even on the streets I would write for hours, most of it incoherent nonsense, my fantasies, my thoughts and my goals. Maybe when I'm dead, I will leave them for the world to read so they can see just how far my mind was lost for many of those years. Once Rebel Ink came along, I no longer felt the need to write them, as for the first time in my life I had a family to confide in. Now, he has convinced me to take back up the pen and write about those years. No matter how painful the memory, he wants me to put it in writing. The trouble is, I can't really remember much about specific events, just a feeling of being scared all the time. He reckons the information is stored in there and to be able to deal with it properly I have to release it. I don't really know if it's a good idea as I have tried so hard to forget about that part of my life. It took me a long time to be convinced to even go see a psychiatrist as I felt it was admitting defeat. At the same time my issues kept cropping up and defeating me on another level. This was evident during my relationship with Billy. He struggled for me to let him get close. He described me as a closed book that had a huge padlock attached and he was afraid that nobody had the key to open it. Of course he was right. No matter how hard he tried, I would get to a certain point and then close up shop. It was Billy who convinced me to go and get professional help and he always said it wasn't for his sake but for my own sanity.

So here it goes. Let me go back to that dark place I swore I would never return to. Even the thoughts of that house makes my stomach tighten in the same knots that was a constant the whole time I lived there. I have only walked past that house once since the authorities removed me. Normally, I would take the long route around to avoid it, but one day roadworks left me with no other choice. As I got close to it that day, I found myself bursting into a run to pass it as quickly as possible. I mean, I don't know what I thought was going to happen. Years had passed, but I suppose the memories had not.

Okay, so I do remember this one time — it must have been close to my seventh birthday because I remember the only thing I wanted was a purple My Little Pony toy. I was obsessed with them, but had yet to ever own one.

As you can imagine, growing up in a crack den, we didn't really have many toys or possessions. In fact, the only thing I remember having was this little woolen brown bear that I had found out by the dumpster one day. I named him Pip and carried him everywhere with me. Even then I knew Pip was at risk of being taken if I had just left him lying around the house. Anyway, I had asked Mom for weeks about getting this specific pony for my birthday. I made it very clear it was the one with bright pink hair and star sparkles. She always made promises she didn't keep, but this time she sat me down, looked into my hopeful blue eyes and promised me I would wake up on the morning of my birthday to a brand new purple My Little Pony with the bright pink hair and star sparkles. I remember feeling true excitement for the first time in my young years. I spent the next few days telling all my friends that I was finally getting one and that I could join them as they gathered their ponies to brush their hair at the school lunch break.

As much as all the stuff that happened at home made me sad, I suppose I was oblivious (or immune) to it, as it was all I ever really knew. But the knowledge of getting this present all for me on the morning of my birthday made me the happiest I had ever known. As I drifted off to sleep each night, my thoughts were only focused on my birthday present. So, a couple of nights before the big day, I was awoken from my sleep by the familiar sound of shouting coming from the kitchen downstairs. The sweet scent that filled my room stung my nostrils as it always did. (I now know that scent was from the crack cocaine being smoked by my mother and numerous partners over the year). I slid out of bed and snuck over to the door to hear what was happening. My mother was crying and angry. I can remember her yelling, "That money was for my baby. I told you that, you scumbag." The arguing continued back and forth and then was followed by a loud slamming of the front door. I sat against the door listening to my mother sob, but I daren't leave my room to go comfort her. Even at the age of six years, I knew that I wasn't going to get my pony.

CHAPTER SEVEN

Rebecca's shoulders hunch up around her ears as my scream reaches her. She glances back at me, her mouth slightly open in bewilderment. The figure in the trench coat doesn't even flinch. My mind turns to offering Rebecca up as a sacrifice while I make my escape. I can't just leave her here, can I? Finally, the tense standoff is broken as Rebecca finally speaks, "What is wrong, Megan?" Her tone is quite demanding for the situation at hand. My focus is not on her but on the tall figure who has slowly started to walk towards us, his hands still buried in his pockets, his face menacing under the flickering glare of the fluorescent hall lights. My feet regain movement as I begin to shuffle backwards, but I daren't break eye contact with the predator looming towards Rebecca. As Rebecca waits for my response, my facial expression causes her to turn and face the figure who is almost upon her now. I wait for him to lunge, to reach out those long arms and grab violently, but he stops. Now that he is closer, his expression has gone from menacing to bemused.

Rebecca turns to me once more. "Megan, this is Detective Roberts." She has clearly realized the situation and tries her best at a forced sympathetic smile and a head tilt. Not for the first time today, I feel so stupid. The rush of blood to my cheeks clearly indicating just how stupid I feel. In an attempt to explain myself, I try to find the words, "Oh my God, I am so sorry. I thought that..." but my explanation is cut short by him.

"There is no need to explain. You've had a traumatic experience today and we are going to do everything we can to help you." The detective's eyes are kind but tired. He looks like he hasn't slept in days. I can smell the coffee off his breath from quite a distance. His thick black hair has begun to grey and I suspect he is a lot younger than his image portrays. I am still using Rebecca as a human shield as he speaks. He takes a step forward and removes one hand from his pocket to reach out and shake mine.

The act of a handshake is believed to have first originated from the cowboys in the West. It was a display to show your enemy that you weren't concealing a gun. I think about this as my shaking hand extends to meet his. *But what about the other hand, Megan? What might that be concealing?* It's good to see my suspicion is still active and my guard held high, but how this random thought popped into my head bewilders me.

"If it's okay with you, we would like to have a little chat with you in your dressing room. It won't take long." I try to place his accent. I reckon it's from Los Angeles, but it sounds like he has moved around quite a bit. I really want to explain myself better, but I just come out with a one-word response of, "Sure."

Rebecca has already set off in front of us and we follow in unison. I am disappointed in myself; if this really was my stalker, then I would have been defenseless. I thought I was stronger than that. Actually, I know I'm stronger than that. As I walk behind the tall frame

Ink Princess

of Roberts, I make a promise to myself that I will be prepared next time anything like that happens. Never again will I be a defenseless victim.

I follow the lieutenant into my dressing room. There are two uniformed cops already standing there. They are arguing over last night's baseball game and our arrival doesn't seem to stop them. It's just another day on the job for these guys. Their flippant attitude to the situation does irk me, and I'm glad when Roberts tells them to "Knock it off," but then he joins them by adding, "Both teams suck anyway." I am used to the 'boy banter' from the shop, but I am in no humor to tolerate it today. Roberts tells me to take a seat and motions to the red velvet covered couch while he pulls up a chair. Straight out of the 'Cop textbook 101', he then flips the chair backwards, resting his lanky arms across the backrest.

"So Megan, I have read your file on the way over here and I can see this issue has been going on quite some time." *No shit, Sherlock* are the words that come to mind. I didn't want to start from the beginning. I had been over this so many times with so many different cops that had been on the case for a few months at a time, before then being transferred to a different precinct. Each time a new detective had been assigned to my case, they would always promise to be the one to catch the guy. I had heard it all before and really didn't have any confidence in him ever being caught at this stage. I hide my frustration and reply with, "Yeah, around seven years now, but this is the first time I have heard him speak."

"Okay, listen, we have attempted to trace the call, but we believe he used what we call a burner phone, untraceable I'm afraid. This guy is smart. Going through the file and the events he has caused you, most amateurs would have slipped up somewhere, but this guy doesn't leave a fingerprint or a hair fiber. Even the paintings he left for you, we couldn't find a trace of his DNA on there. This tells me that we are dealing with a smart and calculating individual. Listen, Megan, I'm going to be honest with you. The powers that be don't see stalkers who haven't physically harmed or even murdered to be a priority in investigations, so I'm sure you have lost any hope of anybody taking you seriously from our side. Well, I am telling you I have experience with this situation, and that's why I was put on the case. I will not rest until we find this creep, and let you get on with your life in peace."

And the Oscar goes to... Detective Roberts. I have to hand it to him, that was some speech. Am I skeptical? Yes. Am I going to refuse his help? No. He is all I have at this moment and I am just going to have to go with it and hope for the best.

"Do you think I am in danger?" It's the only question I want to hear the answer to. I half want to hear the sugar-coated answer that will appease my worries. All of the others would assure me that I was completely safe, but as I was starting to find out, Roberts wasn't like the others. "We are treating this very seriously, Megan. In all of these years hidden in the shadows, he waits until you are on a live TV show to make verbal contact with you. I feel his delusions may be escalating and he may want to take his contact further. I briefly spoke with your manager, Paul, and he assured me this topic was not meant to be brought up. I don't want to scare you any further than you already are, but one thing you will get with me is straight answers. I feel it's imperative for you to have all of the facts up front so you don't leave yourself in vulnerable situations."

Jesus, I wanted sugar-coated; I just got a sour apple taste of truth pie. I liked it. No bullshit – this is what I needed to hear.

"Now, what I'd like to do is check your cell phone. Do you have it with you?" I reach for my bag to retrieve it. As I do, I notice my hands are still rattling with adrenaline. Maybe it's just a gut reaction from years on the job, but I see one of the standing cops slowly moving his hand from his thumb tucked into the front of his belt to covering his side arm. I thought I was the victim here? As I pull my phone out, he studies it and then returns his thumb to the front once more. I somehow feel safer knowing that this guy is on his game.

"Here you go. I have had it switched off since this morning." I push the 'ON' button while handing it over to him. My mind suddenly races as he takes it in his hand. Shit, I hope there are no pictures on there I don't want him to see. A trivial worry amongst the severity of the situation, but a natural reaction when someone else is in control of your cell. I eagle stare as his finger scrolls my menu. To my relief he has gone straight to my messages. As he opens them up, numerous tones of 'ping, ping, ping' ring out in the silent dressing room. He holds the phone at arm's length, as people who need glasses often do.

"Popular woman." His attempt at humor cracks a half smile to my face. "Okay, who have we got here – Zane, Carol, Sammy, Lou, Silly Billy." Roberts flicks his eyes past the phone to confirm these names. My confused face causes him to lower the phone to his knee. What's wrong, Megan?"

"Did you say Sammy?" I knew he had, but I needed confirmation. He resumes the position of the cell to arm's length and squints hard to make out the writing.

"Eh, yes, Sammy, text sent at 3:18pm today. The message is blank though." I feel the bile from my stomach creep up my throat and swallow hard to suppress it coming any further.

"That's impossible. Sammy has been dead for years. Can I see it please?" I knew there was nobody else by the name of Sammy in my phonebook, but I still racked my brains to find the mistake. I also knew it wasn't an old message as I had lost all of them from Sammy when my phone died a watery death in a porcelain water hole (my phone fell into a toilet on a drunken night out). I remember how upset I was that my texts from him were gone. I take my cell from Roberts and examine the glowing screen. My eyes open wide, as there in plain view was the name SAMMY staring back at me from my inbox. A blank message that said more than words could.

"This is impossible. That's Sammy's cell number, but I don't understand. He's been dead over four years." Roberts motions one of the cops over. "We are going to have to take this for our analytics to take a look at." The cop pulls out a small evidence bag and holds it open for me to place inside. The 'pings' continue as he takes it away.

"Don't worry, we will find out how that text got sent and who sent it, but for now I want you staying off any cell phones or social media." How has this day gone so bad? I actually feel like I am in a movie. I just hope the script has a '...and then she woke up; it was all a dream' ending. Somehow, I don't think so. I should be feeling relieved that the interview was over; after weeks of worry and anticipation this should be a time of celebration. Instead, I sit here confused and terrified to my core.

"Do you think this guy has Sammy's phone? But if he does, like how did he get it? I don't understand." I knew my question sounded stupid, but I really wanted an answer as my head could not get around it.

"It's a possibility, Megan, but at this stage I really don't have an answer for you. As soon as I do, I will come to you directly." I wanted to scream, "Do you even know who Sammy is? Have you done your research, Mr. Big Shot Detective?" But once again, I stay silent consumed with overbearing thoughts racing through my mind. I feel annoyed that I didn't get to read the texts sent by my friends. I was going to be lost without my cell. My fear is replaced with anger that all of this has been caused by the actions of one mentally disturbed human being, I try to convince myself that if he was here right now I would punch him straight in the nose. *Weren't so brave in the hallway when you thought it was him, now were you, Megan?* Subconscious always calls me on my bullshit. My mental ramblings are interrupted by Roberts.

"Okay, so if it's alright with you, we are going to arrange a police escort back to your apartment and I am going to leave these two guys with you for the night, purely as a precaution. This guy may be deluded, but I really don't think he would be stupid enough to try anything tonight." One of the cops speaks for the first time to confirm Roberts' words, "Don't worry, no one will get anywhere near you while we are there." He puffs out his already rounded chest as he speaks – a display of a macho protector, but it does make me feel better. Roberts stands up;

his lanky frame towers over the two robust cops. My plans of meeting up with the guys from the shop later have clearly gone out the window. I don't even have my cell to contact anyone.

As we step back out into the hallway, I know that I am now walking out into the unknown. I wish Billy was here. I wish for his arm around my shoulder and for him to tell me everything was going to be alright. In this moment I realized just how much I missed him. I follow Roberts, and the two cops strategically follow close behind me. We make our way to the back entrance fire doors. Roberts stops, peering out through the glass to make sure the coast is clear.

It is now pitch black outside and the rain has turned to a delicate snow. As the doors are pushed open, the cool breeze hits my face. It feels amazing to breath fresh air again. As soon as we step out, there is a large flash of a camera pointed in our direction. I can't see, but I'm sure my trigger happy cop has reached for his gun behind me. I can see the headlines now 'Cop Guns Down Paparazzi in Mistaken Identity.'

As we walk up the slope and towards the street, the flashes start to multiply, as more and more cameramen rush over to our location. A TV camera gets pushed up to my face while a journalist barks questions, "Megan, tell us, do you have any idea of the identity of your stalker? Are you in fear of your life? Will this mean the end of *Rebel Ink* for you now?"

Her questions go unanswered as I am being rushed through the crowd of photographers, but it doesn't faze her and she continues, this time trying to get an answer from Roberts, "Do you have any lead suspects in the case, detective?" A true veteran at this stage, he just replies with a deadpan, "No comment." Finally, we reach the parked cop

Ink Princess

car. I climb in the back; as the door is shut the noise from the overzealous reporter fades out. I instinctively put my hand over my face to shield myself from the blinding camera flashes. My two new personal cop escorts both get in and start up the engine. "Bloody animals," one of them says in his thick New York accent.

The driver lets out a short bleat of his siren to clear the path of paparazzi surrounding the car and we slowly take off. I am relieved to be getting out of there, but then of course my paranoia kicks in. What if these two cops are in on it, you know, like dirty cops? They could have struck a deal with my tormenter for a nice little pay off to have me hand delivered to his doorstep. Clearly I have watched too many movies, but you just never know.

I feel I have to break the silence, "So, what are your guys' names?" I try to sound as pleasant as possible, but it comes out like I am questioning them, just in case any shit goes down. The passenger cop speaks, "I'm Marty, and this fat son of a bitch is Carl." Carl raises his hand in a mock backhand slap. "Who you calling fat? I'm not the one whose pants split last week while chasing down a perp, am I?" He lets out a snarling laugh, then checks his rearview mirror to see if I find him as funny as he clearly does himself. I do let out a giggle.

"Don't listen to this guy. He once went to a Weight Watchers class and they threw him out. They said he was a lost cause." The man I now know as Marty is clearly the one with the thickest New York accent possible. I am enjoying the distraction of their banter.

"It's not your fault, though," Carl retorts.

"What's not my fault?" Marty asks knowing an insult is building.

"That you're so fat."

"Why's it not my fault?"

"I blame your mama. She's so fat, when she left the house in high heels she came back wearing flip flops." This time all three of us burst out laughing. These guys had the typical cop buddy bromance going on and it was kind of cute to watch.

"Don't you talk about my mama like that. You know she will kick your ass." Marty pretends to be offended after his initial laughter. Marty and Carl actually look like they could be brothers. Both sport crew cuts and share similar body shapes. I daren't point out their similarities as I could predict their reaction already. After the brief pantomime joking between the two, I no longer believe they are criminal masterminds working in cahoots with my stalker. As the conversation ceases, my mind returns to the Sammy text. There is just no plausible way a text could have been sent from his phone. Even if Jane, Sammy's wife, had the phone, surely it would be dead by now. Maybe, it was just a delayed network error, but I know it can't be as I have had to change my number numerous times since Sammy's death.

I notice peering faces trying to get a glimpse of the criminal residing in the back of the cop car as we pass by. I have to admit, a part of me feels bad ass. Carl pulls the humming cruiser up in front of my apartment block. Spike, my building's front door security, looks concerned at the sight of it.

"Wait here a moment," Carl says as he gets out and walks over to Spike. I watch as Carl explains the situation. I gently wave from my backseat as Spike glances in my direction, but Spike is in his late sixties, so his eyesight isn't what it used to be and he fails to see me. After a minute or so, Carl walks over to open my door.

"Okay Megan, I have had a word with the door gentleman here and he knows the story. We are going to escort you up to your apartment now." Carl cocks his head like a meerkat and studies the street up and down to make sure the coast is clear for me to exit. Spike smiles warmly as I approach him. Spike is an African American, always impeccably dressed in his red turncoat uniform; his gold buttons always shine bright and a large black top hat adorns his head at all times. I have had many conversations with Spike as he has hailed me numerous taxis. He always offers help with bags and holds the door open for you. He is an old school gentleman, and has remained on these doors for over forty years, something he is extremely proud about.

"Miss. Banks, so nice to see you." I have tried insisting he calls me Megan, but a proper gentleman would never dream of it.

"Hey Spike, I hope you are staying warm out of this snow." I genuinely make a fuss over him as many of the female residents do, making sure he has a coffee and something to eat is a daily question I ask him. In all the years he has stood here, he has faced racism, rudeness and abuse, yet he never has a bad word to say about anybody. He just has a good heart.

"Oh, don't you worry about me, young lady. I'm sorry to hear about your trouble, but don't you worry. Nobody will get past my door while I am on duty." His words sound confident and defensive. It brings a smile to my face.

"Aw, thanks Spike. It's just been one of those days, but I will be okay." I don't believe my lie, and neither does he. Marty joins us, and we make our way into the lobby and towards the elevators.

"Okay, so we are going to be outside your apartment door for the night. If you need anything, just knock on your door and we will confirm it is okay to open it up." In the bright lights of the elevator, I now notice Carl speaks from the side of his mouth. The reason for this may be due to the large scar that runs from the corner of his thick lip to just under his nose bone. I desperately want to ask what happened, but deem it inappropriate and return my eyes to his as I meekly answer, "Okay, thank you."

The elevator doors open as we reach my floor. Marty steps out first to inspect the hallway. "Let's go, guys." As uncomfortable as I feel having two cops escorting me down a hallway that I have walked hundreds of times alone, I am still glad they are here. I scan my security card on the little white box outside my apartment. The light turns green and the door unlocks. Before my hand has time to reach for the handle, Carl proceeds to open it and makes the first entrance. "Just wait there one minute. I want to take a quick look around."

As he leaves me and Marty standing at the door, I can hear my guard cat calling out to him. Jake has a 'meow' to rival a small dog. He has woken me many mornings with it, looking for his breakfast. Itchy trigger finger scenarios play out in my head again. *Please don't shoot my cat, mistaking him for a predator!* I am relieved to see Jake has made his way towards me standing at the door. My voice tone immediately changes to a high pitched squeaky one. I am convinced all animal owners adopt this tone at some time or another, the same way adults speak to a baby.

"Aw, hey mister, did you miss me? You must be starving, huh?" I drop to my knees to give him a scratch behind his ears. He purrs as he rubs against my hand. "Cute cat," Marty says in a slightly sleazy way. Carl appears in the hallway. "All clear, come on in." I pick up Jake and make my way into the kitchen. Carl and Marty both begin checking the windows as I prepare Jake's dinner.

"Everything seems fine here, Megan. We are going to leave you to it, but we will be just outside if you need us." I feel sorry for the guys having to stand outside all night, but there is no way I would be staying here if they weren't. As they make their way back out to the hallway, I gently close the door and thank them again.

I rest my head against the door. Tears begin to well up inside me. I fight to hold them back but don't succeed in holding them in. I feel scared, I feel alone, I feel defeated. I hold my hand over my mouth as I really don't want Carl or Marty to hear me sobbing. I wish I had my phone. Zane would know the right words to say right now. Through my clouded, teary eyes, Jake appears at my feet, his face full of concern. 'What's wrong, Mommy?' He follows me closely as I make my way into my bedroom. I let my body flop down onto the soft duvet. Jake swiftly follows; he tucks in under my chin, his cat food breath still fresh from his tasty dinner. I don't expect to sleep tonight, but as my eyes close I find myself drifting further and further into the open arms of slumber.

CHAPTER EIGHT

I wake with a bolt of adrenaline coursing through my body. I am cold and damp with sweat. Jake is still fast asleep on my pillow, curled up and purring. I have no idea what time it is. I feel totally disorientated. My crazy nightmares have been blurred into the reality of yesterday. My body lets me know it needs food by letting a large growl from my stomach, but I feel too sick to eat. Jake stirs as I swing my legs down by the side of the bed. I am still in yesterday's clothes. I feel anxious to get out of them. I need to get the stench of yesterday off my body. I need a shower.

The light is creeping through the curtains, that early morning hazy light. Rubbing the crust from my eyes as I walk to the kitchen, I contemplate whether to check on my two personal security guards outside or just head straight for the shower. I am curious to see if they are still there, but I am embarrassed to let anyone see me in this state. A shower first and then I will plan for the day.

I hurry to the bathroom as the cold wooden floors sting my bare feet. The woolly bathroom mat feels good between my toes. Taking a look in the mirror confirms my decision to wait and shower first was the right one. Yesterday's makeup is congealed and thick black mascara is smudged down my cheeks. As I get to work on removing the mess with numerous make up wipes, my thoughts turn to the drama of the day before. I am desperate to talk to Paul and the guys at the shop. I just want this feeling of being so desperately alone to go away.

I step into the shower and the water hits my skin hard; immediate relief fills my body and my mind. I use double the amount of shower gel and shampoo required, scrubbing yesterday's trauma off my body. As I finally turn the knob off, I stand here while the drops of water leave my body. I don't know how long I have been in here for, but it seems like an eternity. I examine my arms; they have turned a bright red from the scalding water. My image is blurred through the steamed mirror, but I feel like me again. It's small progress, but it's progress, and that's a good start.

As I get dressed and brush the knots out of my hair, I feel presentable enough to check on Carl and Marty. I make my way to the front door but then stop myself as I reach for the handle. What if they have been murdered and my stalker is standing there waiting to pounce? *Get a grip, Megan.* My already paranoid mind has now gone into overdrive and I suspect it will remain that way for quite some time. The irony doesn't escape me as I knock on the door from the inside and wait for a response. The delay makes my breath stop in anticipation, but finally a voice emerges from behind the solid door.

"Hey Megan, this is officer McAdams. Are you okay?" This does nothing for my suspicions as I wanted to hear the voices of my newfound cop friends. I have to ask, "Where's Carl and Marty?"

"Oh, their shift finished an hour ago, so they sent me over as a replacement." I have seen way too many movies. *Open that door and you are dead, Megan.* I mean, I have no obligation to open the door. Most victims in movies are killed because they don't want to be rude, and they invite strangers into their home out of politeness.

"Can you pass me some identification under the door, please?" *Clever girl, Megan.* I can hear him let out a sigh as his belt rattles while he searches for his wallet. He pushes it under the door as instructed. I snatch it up in my fingertips to examine it. Charlie McAdams, born in Michigan 1992; from his photo he looks like a handsome young man, strong chin and sallow skin. It's enough to satisfy my doubts, and I open the door. Much to my relief, I am greeted by the same face from the identification card, but this time the face is wearing a warm smile. I blush as his good looks remind me that I'm not wearing any makeup.

"I'm sorry about that. I'm still a bit freaked out from yesterday."

"That's okay, you are right to be cautious. I spoke with the guys before they left. There were no incidents last night to report." He looks like he should be in college wearing a basketball uniform, not a cop's uniform. His cute face makes me think the streets are going to eat him up fast. *Judgmental as ever, Megan.* I can't help my analyses of people that I meet. "Would you like a cup of coffee?" I offer out of politeness, but I'm not even sure I even have any in my cupboards. Luckily, he declines.

"I'm all good, thanks. I just had one on the way over here." I feel like I should invite him in, but that just feels weird.

"So, is it okay for me to leave today? I am supposed to be at the shop at twelve." It feels strange asking permission, but I suppose there is nothing normal about this situation.

"Detective Roberts will be here at ten. He wants to have a chat with you and then it's his call, I'm afraid" The rebellious street girl side of me kicks up as I think, *And what you going to do about it if I try and leave, Officer McAdams?* I know it's for my own good and he is just doing his job, but what can I say? I'm feisty.

"Okay, I will just wait for him then, thanks." As I close the door and turn the lock, I can't help but feel like a prisoner in my own home. My offer of coffee to McAdams has now made me want one. I smile as I open the cupboard and find I do actually have a jar. My life is so hectic these days, I normally grab a coffee to go on the way to the shop and rarely have time to prepare one by myself. Damn, I should have asked McAdams what time it was. Strange that only now with the absence of my cell do I realize I don't have any clocks in the apartment. I suppose on the streets I never had one either, but I could still tell the hours of the day by streetlights flicking on or off, or the work hour rush to and fro.

My laptop – like a light bulb turning on in my head. Why had I not thought of this already? As I leave the kettle to boil, I go to retrieve it, feeling a little excited to make contact with my loved ones. I open it up and a large digital 8:14am flashes up. Perfect amount of time to check my mail before Roberts gets here. As I open up my Twitter page, I quickly realize that it won't be enough time. Thousands of tweets and messages fill my page. I scroll down quickly reading through them. So far all of them are words of positivity from the interview and support for my stalker situation. As with anybody in the limelight, there are always the haters out there. I try not to let it affect me, but sometimes it can cut you deep.

The keyboard warriors don't hold back from behind the safety of their computer screens. As I get further down, I am relieved to see kind and thoughtful comments flood my page. And then my love bubble is burst as a hater pops up. 'I hope that guy gets his hands on you and slits your throat, do us all a favor #killthebitch' My smile fades as the words battle with my vulnerable state. I know whoever posted that is doing it to get some attention or maybe they just find me really annoying, but they have no idea how it makes me feel. As with all the haters and their nasty comments, they never have anything to say to my face – fucking cowards.

That one comment causes me to click out of Twitter and into my emails. I find my inbox is equally full. I scroll down through the numerous emails and smile as the familiar names that I want to see are all there. As soon as I see Zane's name, I click it open first. Roberts would probably be peeved with me being online, but I needed this.

Hey Honey,

I tried your cell, but I can't seem to get ahold of you. So, I headed over to your place but Spike said you weren't allowed any visitors. I don't want you being alone, so as soon as you can, contact me, and I can meet you anywhere. I will be at the shop from 10am tomorrow. I presume you want to cancel your 12 o'clock appointment, but I will wait until the morning to do anything. You know we are thinking about you and just like before we will get through it as a family.

Love,

Zane x

I get emotional as I read his words. I wish he was here to give me one of his huge bear hugs. The next email I click open is from Billy.

Hi baby,
I can't believe this fucking guy. I am so angry right now I swear if I got my hands on him I would make him pay for what he has done to you. I tried calling you, but you must not have your phone. I watched the show tonight. I was so proud of you, you killed it! I am gigging in San Francisco tonight, but if you need me for anything, just call me.
Billy

His words of protection make me feel better about the situation, as it always did when we were together. But, as kind as his words are, I can't get over the 'Hi baby'. It makes me sad that he still calls me that. I am no longer his baby, no matter how much I wish I was right now. I know my emotions are running high right now, so I realize it is not the time to reach out to Billy and have him back in my life. I hit the reply button but sit staring at a blank screen not knowing what to say. As I try to word what I want to say in my head, my thoughts are interrupted by a new email flashing up on my screen. I click on the icon.

What appears on my screen makes time stand still; a white noise filled with nausea rings around my head. I blink down hard and shake my head, as if some way this will change the writing I see on the screen in front of me: 1 new email from Sammy. My hands tremble and sweat. A sick curiosity to open the message battles with my instinct to close the laptop and wait until Roberts is here to open it. I really don't think anyone in my position could resist the urge to know how the hell their best friend who has been dead for four years is now contacting them through text and email. The subject box is empty and the email is definitely Sammy's. I close my eyes as my finger pushes the enter button. I open them to a squint to examine my screen.

Dearest Megan,
I WILL NEVER LEAVE YOU.

My reaction is not one I was expecting. I burst out into an uncontrollable laughter. Maybe this is the moment that I finally lose my mind, the years of turmoil finally cracking what's left of my sanity. Maybe its best I return to the streets, go off grid before they come take me away to the nut house. I stand up and compose myself to a certain degree of normality. Oblivious to my previous protocol of precautions, I head to my front door and swing it open violently. McAdams jumps up straight from his leaned position against the wall. He is clearly startled, as his eyes are opened much wider than before.

"Get Roberts over here now." My voice comes with authority for the first time in the last twenty-four hours.

"What's wrong, Megan?" he asks, half trying to remain a cop, but his genuine concern as a person is evident.

"Just please get him over here as soon as possible." My voice is softer now but still exasperated.

"Okay, I will call now and see where he is." I feel he knows not to push me on the reason I want him here. I leave him to make the call and return inside. In times like this I would usually turn to my painting as a therapeutic release, but I can't even find the energy to attempt it right now. Instead, I slide down against my kitchen wall, pulling my knees in tight with my arms wrapped around them. The light from my open laptop still flickers from the kitchen table. I bury my head down to avoid eye contact with it.

I wasn't asleep, but I wasn't fully awake either as a knock wakes me from a trance. I am still in my huddled position on the kitchen floor. I have no idea how long I have been waiting, but my limbs ache as I rise to my feet. My left foot has been starved of blood and that horrible feeling of pins and needles pricks and prods as I try to walk towards my hallway. The feeling of waking up with no feeling in my arms or feet is up there amongst my worst fears. Others include turning on a light switch in the dark and the bulb blows leaving you helpless, running out of gas on a secluded back road in the middle of the night, and the battery dying on your cell phone on said secluded back road makes that situation even worse. I am also extremely claustrophobic. This condition was forced upon me as one of my mother's 'lovely' boyfriends locked me in a cupboard at the age of five while he entertained some drug dealers. He then got high and forgot I was in there until the next day. Well, actually I like to think he forgot. Maybe he just didn't care. So, add enclosed spaces to my basket case. Maybe they should come and take me away.

I open the door and Roberts is standing there; the black circles under his eyes look darker today. His stubble is thicker and fuller. I imagine shaving is just a hassle for him and he avoids it until a full beard grows.

"Morning Megan, I got here as soon as I could." his voice sounds like he has been drinking hard liquor last night. Just what I need, a stereotypical divorced, insomniac, alcoholic detective.

"Come in." I feel like I have been assigned another deadbeat to my case and my patience has worn thin. As we reach the kitchen, my observation skills are confirmed as I can now smell the whiskey emulating from his breath. As much as I want to blurt out my information, I sarcastically mutter, "I think you need a coffee," and give him a look to make sure he knows that I am not impressed with his state. He looks sheepish and embarrassed by my comment and just nods his head in agreement. As I prepare two cups and wait for the kettle to boil, he begins to open his files and lay them out on the countertop.

"So why did you ask me over here, Megan? Did something happen?" As I jump to answer, I am reminded that an 'I told you so' is coming my way for going on social media against Roberts' advice.

"Yeah, so I know you said to stay off my social media, but this morning I checked my emails and as I was reading through some of them a new email came through. It was from Sammy again. I totally freaked out." He knows the blame game has now shifted on to me and regains his confident posture.

"Listen, I understand why you wanted to check your emails, but I really wished you hadn't. I went through Sammy's file from the night he died. There was no cell phone recovered. I spoke with his widow, eh, Jane, and she doesn't know where it is and reckons he was never without it. So whoever this creep is, somehow he has Sammy's phone and now he is trying to scare you by using it. I feel he is extremely tech savvy and the reports back from our analysis team unfortunately don't leave any trace back to him but do confirm that it is his cell." I am relieved to hear Roberts has actually done some work and presented me with some answers to my burning questions.

"But how the hell did this creep get his hands on Sammy's phone? And if he has had it all this time, why is he only using it now?" I know these are rhetorical at this stage, but I still need to ask.

"Don't worry, we are looking into it and as soon as we find out I will let you know."

"And what am I supposed to do in the meantime?"

"I know it's hard, but the best thing you can do is just return to your daily routine. If you go down the route of hiding out, trust me, I have seen it drive people demented. We are not going to let this guy win, Megan. He has escalated his advances towards you and this leaves him open to being caught. Whether yesterday's phone call was premeditated or not, he has made himself publically known. For years, he has stayed hidden, but now he can't control his delusions and he has broken the barriers that he had clearly set himself. In my experience, this is when these guys get caught. We will find him, Megan."

I have to admit his words win me over for the second time. He talks a good one, but it remains to be seen if he can back it up. "But, if his delusions are escalating doesn't that mean I am at more risk now than ever before?" I can see he is impressed or maybe relieved to be dealing with someone that is actually clued into the situation and not in complete denial like some might be in my shoes.

"I'm not going to lie to you. Yes, you are right. There is an added risk that he might step it up further and approach you, but to be honest that's what we are counting on. Don't get me wrong, your safety is our main concern, but this guy is crafty. I think our best chance is luring him in to make contact in person and that's when we grab the guy."

Now I begin to wonder if Roberts is a loose cannon. Is this the reason he was transferred? Is this his first time using this technique or have many attempts failed before me? Either way I don't really have a choice. I need to find some trust in his method. This is the guy they have given me, so I have to suck it up and go with it. I try to find words to reassure him that I am onboard.

"Okay, whatever it takes to get this guy out of my life, I am willing to try. I just need to know that I am safe." I emphasize the word 'need' and not just 'want'. For my own sanity, I need somebody to tell me I would be okay.

"We won't let anything happen to you, Megan." His use of 'we' is deflecting the blame off himself personally if anything does happen to me. Roberts then reaches into the inside pocket of his oversized trench coat and pulls out my cell. I gladly take it from him.

"Now, I suggest you change your number as soon as possible. We have checked it out and there is nothing we are concerned about as regards to the phone, but this guy obviously has your cell number, so it's best to get it changed." I don't bother to tell him how many times I have had my number changed in the last few years. Instead I just nod in agreement while I examine my screen to see all the missed calls and messages I had received while they had it.

"Do you want a lift anywhere?" His words disrupt my frantic scrolling.

"Well, actually, I have a tattoo appointment at twelve. Do you think I should do it?"

"I actually think it would be good for you. As I said, let's keep your routine as normal as possible. One thing I will say to you is not to talk to the press. There will be plenty looking to get the full story from you, but this can be detrimental to our case. You saw how quickly it escalated when it was brought up on live TV. He wants to feel acknowledged. Let's not give him that privilege." I am relieved to hear I will be tattooing today. I know I will feel better once I have my machine in my hand and am surrounded by my family at the shop. I gather my things up as fast as I can and follow Roberts out. As scary and miserable as this whole experience has been, I can't help but feel a little bit excited. I think I have experienced every emotion possible in the last twenty-four hours, but I know there is a lot more to come.

CHAPTER NINE

We pull up outside the shop; our electric neon blue sign shines bright through the slanted rain. Rebel Ink can be seen from a couple of blocks away. I am always happy to see that sign; it means that I am only a few feet away from my sanctuary inside. Huddled on the steps in the spilling rain are a small group of paparazzi and local news crew. I almost feel sorry for them being out in these conditions, but at the same time I know they would sell you out without a moment's hesitation. Roberts feels the need to remind me of his instructions once more before we get out. I suppose he has just cause as I blatantly ignored his requests quite recently.

"Now, like I said, Megan, please don't speak to any reporters or even speak about the situation with your customers, okay?" He can't help sounding paternal and I can't help feeling defiant. I don't reply but nod my head in an act of reluctant conformity. The photographers haven't noticed our arrival, but as soon as the car door cracks open they are alert and cameras are hastily being readied. Flashes boom as they descend the steps like locusts. The familiar orders are barked from the assemble, voices are distorted from the rainfall. I pull my hood up as I try to push through them. Our two regular door security guys, Rob and Steve, come to my rescue and they start pulling the eager photographers out of my path. I hear bits and pieces from the barrage of questions being asked simultaneously, as I rush by.

"Megan, have they caught him yet?"

"What's next?"

"Hey man, get your hands off of me."

"Can we get a statement?"

"Megan, look this way."

Finally, I make it to the front door. Steve opens it while Rob makes himself a human shield around me. The full front window of the shop is covered with a grey tint, which allows us to see out but nobody can see in. This is for our customers' privacy but also to keep prying eyes away while we are filming for the show. As Steve closes and locks the door, I am relieved to have the barrier of concealment between us and them. It doesn't dissuade them from continuing the barrage of camera flashes that penetrate the tinted glass.

"Thanks guys, I don't think I would have gotten through them without your help." Steve and Rob are man mountains. They look like they were born in the wrong era, both sporting Viking-like beards and arms bigger than my entire head. Their similarity in stature is purely coincidental, but they look like they would have belonged with the same tribe going to war. Each stands well over six foot and their width makes navigating through doorways difficult.

"No problem, Megan. They are fucking vultures." Rob talks exactly the way you would expect from a man of his size too, low, deep and gravely.

"One pipsqueak was threatening to sue me for putting my hands on him." Steve, on the other hand, does not talk exactly the way you would expect from a man of his size. His tone is high pitched, fast paced and a lisp makes his words slur. When he speaks, his intimidation percentage definitely drops down, but you still wouldn't mess with this bear like man.

The hum of tattoo machines can be heard over the drum and bass music gently pulsating from the shop's speakers. There is no better sound in the world to me than a finely tuned tattoo machine vibrating in unison with the artist in control. It is an almost trance like sound. It relaxes me and takes my mind off to a faraway place. Sometimes, I wish I could just stay there, but I always end up coming back. The smell of green soap and disinfected floors fills my nostrils; this smell has often been described as addictive from tattoo customers across the world. You can tell a lot from a studio just from the initial smell that greets you as you walk in. We are often complimented on how good our studio smells. If a tattoo shop smells clean, you are off to a good start as a customer. Obviously there is way more to it than that, but you can gain a client's trust right from the start.

I always say one of the best traits somebody can have working in the body modification world is obsessive compulsive disorder. You need to obsess about cleanliness – the more paranoid and anal you are about sterilization the better. This condition also improves you as an artist, making sure every single detail of the procedure is to your highest possible ability. But as I mentioned during my interview, it can also drive a person demented putting the pressure of perfection on yourself. Our studio is always spotless and it's not just because we are under the scrutiny of television cameras. It has always been like this. Lou set out a standard, and that standard just does not get broken. It makes me beam with pride when a customer compliments our level of cleanliness.

Our shop here in New York looks quite minimal compared to the Boston one. Lou went for clean white walls with strategic art placed in a Zen like fashion throughout. Black leather couches and a large television screen make up the waiting area. It is an open plan, so we work side by side with no divides (we have curtain partitions if somebody is getting a private area tattooed). This makes it a lot easier for the cameras to move around when we are shooting, something Lou had considered when designing the layout. The piercing and sterilization rooms are closed off at the back of the shop. It does look lovely, but I still prefer the old school look of our Boston shop. Sailor Jerry Flash hanging on the walls amongst countless stencil designs gives it the feeling of a true artist's shop.

I make my way to our reception area. I feel tentative as I walk, like I am a stranger walking into the shop for the first time. Much to my relief, I spot Zane coming out from the back room. I stride towards him and throw my arms around his neck. A deeper embrace than I have experienced in my life. It feels good to hold somebody that I care about. Zane is not used to seeing me displaying emotion in this manner. I am usually so reserved. This new hugging Megan feels strange to me.

"It's so good to see you, Megan. I have been worried sick." His bearded chin tickles my ear as he speaks.

"I'm fine, just glad to be here now." He knows I am lying and as he pulls away from our hug, his look lets me know that there is no need to lie to him.

"It's just all been a whirlwind of craziness," I say in way of an explanation. The tattoo machine buzzing stops as the guys spot me, my brothers, my protectors. Lou, Mike and Trent take their gloves off and walk over to me and we head into the staff room. Their faces are all serious. They look worried and pissed off at the same time. Shit, amongst all the distraction of my stalker, I suddenly become paranoid that I had said something on the show to let these guys down. I hadn't even thought much about the actual interview as my mind was clouded with worry. Lou places his broad hand on my shoulder. Lou is not a hugger, so this is about as close as he gets to one.

"You alright, kid?" Here I go again, the tears welling up. I fight to hold them back. I think the floodgates that have remained locked for so many years have been opened up and I can't seem to close them again. I just nod my head as I know if I open my mouth those tears are coming out. It's strange; the guys have always known me to be a strong individual, not showing any weakness in the face of adversity, and I don't want to show them that this has mentally broken me. Frankie boy joins us just as Mike is about to speak.

"We are all really proud of you, girl. The way you handled the whole thing was amazing. You killed the interview and represented us artists in the best possible way. You must have been reading up on the dictionary because I have never heard you so articulate." We all burst out laughing at Mike's joke. As my face cracks with laughter the tears come pouring out. The result is a snotty mess of laughter and crying. Zane puts one arm back around my shoulder and gently shakes me.

"It's okay, Megan. We won't let anything happen you." I feel embarrassed as I wipe the tears with my sleeve. At least Mike's words have somewhat appeased my worries about letting the guys and the shop down.

I spend the next half hour reiterating the events of yesterday as best I can remember. It feels good to let them know exactly what happened. For the most part the guys just let me talk, rarely stopping me to ask questions. As I speak, things become clearer in my head. It's like getting all this information out has allowed space for me to think again. Their reactions vary from confusion to anger and everything in between. Unsurprisingly they are most shocked by the messages from Sammy's phone. Just like me they can't get their heads around it. I do my best to explain everything but find myself reassuring them that it's all under control. Maybe subconsciously I do it to reassure myself also.

After I have poured my heart and soul out, there seems to be no words left from anybody. A somber silence hangs in the air of our shop's staff room. I choose the right words to break the awkwardness, "So come on, whose hairy ass was that?" We all laugh as the visual memory surfaces in our minds once again. I don't get a direct answer, just suspicious looks and knowing glances passed between them. I know the guys have more questions, but right now they are questions I don't even have the answers to. I order them back to work and assure them I am okay. Zane comes over to tell me my customer has arrived for her appointment early. Understandably, she is wondering if she is still getting tattooed today.

"Shannon is here for her twelve appointment. Are you sure you are still up for doing it? She seems totally cool if you are not." I have thought about it all morning; I would never put a client at risk if I wasn't one hundred percent sure that I can give them my utmost best. It's a strict rule in the shop that nobody works if they are hungover. The customer is paying for your skills and your time. If you are dehydrated with a banging headache, you are not giving them the best version of you, and that can affect the quality of their tattoo that they have to wear for the rest of their life.

"No, it's fine, I want to do it. Just tell her I will be out in a minute. Thanks Zane." I am confident I can get my head in the game and pull off a killer tattoo. Tattooing is my therapy. I suppose it's an addiction. I crave my machine if I am away from it for more than a day. I miss the smell, miss the noise, miss the adrenaline. Withdrawals – maybe I am more like my mother than I thought. I take a deep breath in and slowly exhale out. The voice in my head tells me I can do this, that inner dialogue pep talk we all give ourselves when we're nervous, or maybe that's just me? Game face on, I walk out confident and smiling,

"Hi Shannon, thanks for coming in today." As I shake her hand I realize that I am over compensating for the situation at hand. Shannon is sweet and polite, but there it is, right there in her eyes. That look, that look that I hate – the look of pity. As we make small talk, it quickly dawns on me that I am now condemned to talk about the one thing I have avoided talking about for the last seven years for the foreseeable future with customers who have that look of pity in their eyes. I keep my cool and move on to the tattoo. I already have her design drawn up; preparation is key in this game, but even preparation can be thrown a curveball as customers can have a last minute change of mind on the day. Thankfully, I tend to avoid this by being thorough during the consultation process.

Zane hands me the drawing I have done to show Shannon. Jesus, I hope she is happy with it. Today would not be a good day for a curveball. She wanted a 'Lucky Chinese Cat', right up my alley style wise. We discussed the color options and meanings behind it, fine tuning details like if the left paw is the waving one it will attract customers to your business, but if it's the right it's for good fortune and wealth. When she told me she was getting it because her daughter had just recovered from meningitis, I knew it had to be green for good health and white for happiness and good things to come. It's these kind of details that can make a regular image tattoo that bit more personal for the customer, and by the end of the consultation I will have written down all our brainstorming information so I can incorporate it into the design.

Placement is also really important and this can determine the dimensions and style of the tattoo. Luckily she wants this one on the side of her thigh, a perfect place for this design. As I show Shannon what I have drawn up, I hold my breath in anticipation.

"Oh my God, I love it. Honestly, it's just amazing. I can't wait to have it on me." Relieved, I head over to my station to begin setting up, leaving an excited Shannon chatting with Zane. He would make anybody who was nervous totally relaxed with his laidback smiling demeanor.

It feels good to be back at my station. I feel in control again. I set up my equipment with surgical precision. My obsessive nature dictates that everything is laid out evenly and all facing the same direction. I am most careful when pouring out my ink into the tattoo cups. One drop spilled and I have to start all over again. Obviously there is proper protocol to follow to avoid cross contamination, but I do drive Lou crazy with the amount of times I change my gloves before even getting to the tattoo. He often mocks that he is taking the cost of the gloves out of my wages. I just can't do it any other way. Even when I was living on the streets, everything I owned was neatly packed away and never messy. As the saying goes, 'a clean house, a clear mind'. The lack of the house part didn't stop me abiding by this rule.

I set out my ink cups like a tiny army of color soldiers, all lined up and ready for action. I always put a little of every color out as I like to experiment with mixing as I go. Some I won't even use during the tattoo, but I like to have that option there. That's the fun part about being an artist – once you know your color palettes, you can try new things and push yourself further every time, whether it's on paper or on skin.

I will always set up at least three tattoo machines, one liner and two shaders, depending on the tattoo. I can have up to five machines set up. I am lucky that the guys at the shop are machine builders, so most of mine have been custom built for me and always run perfectly. A proper machine can make or break a tattoo artist.

The shop buzzes with excitement around me. I can't help but notice the staring in my direction from customers getting worked on. I know it's just curiosity on their part, but it is making me feel really uncomfortable. I try to block it out and continue with my mental checklist as I prepare for the tattoo that is going to take me around five hours. My everyday tasks almost trick my brain into believing that this is a normal day. In between the adrenaline rushes, my stomach rumbles at the lack of food, but as soon as I allow myself to feel the hunger, it is quickly replaced with nausea. I call Shannon over, again forcing the best smile I can.

"You ready for this?" I ask somewhat rhetorically. Shannon is chirpy in nature. "Oh yes, I can't Wait." (That's what they all say until the pain kicks in). She has changed into her shorts, which allows me to place the stencil on straight away. Her legs are quite wide and the skin is already stretched tight. This makes it easier for me to tattoo as I don't have to keep as much of a stretch on the skin with my free hand.

I step back to examine the purple stencil and make sure I am happy with the position and flow on her thigh. As you can probably guess, I am very particular about how the tattoo sits on the skin. One of the worst mistakes an artist can do is trying to stencil a tattoo on a customer who is already sitting or lying down. The tattoo should be straight when standing up. Unusually for me, I am happy with this one first go.

"Okay girl, go have a look in the mirror and tell me what you think." This is a request that us artists do out of politeness more than anything. It is our job to know where the tattoo goes and if it fits right. You will always have customers who can be awkward and get you to move it thinking they know better, but this almost always results in them agreeing to move it back to the original placement you had suggested.

"Oh yes, I love it," is the response from the ever enthused Shannon. I have a feeling that even if it was upside down she would still 'love it'.

"Yeah, it's going to look awesome, girl, so I'm going to get you to lie on your side and try to get as comfortable as possible. We will start with some small lines to ease you in. If you want me to stop or take a break at any stage, you just let me know." As I rhyme off my polite routine, I can't help but worry that Shannon may be a chatterbox. I don't mind a bit of conversation throughout the tattoo, but constant rambling can be very distracting when you are trying to concentrate. As she awkwardly shuffles up on to the bed and gets into position, I open my disposable needles and tubes. It's always at this last stage that I begin to get excited for the tattoo. Even after hundreds of times, I still feel the rush of getting to do what I love most as my job.

One final glove change and I am ready to begin. As I hit my foot pedal the machine gently hums and vibrates in my hand. This junkie is getting her fix; this is what I crave. I crack a little smile to myself. After all the craziness from the last few days, holding my machine in my hand makes everything seem better.

The next five and half hours fall into a vortex of time. When I am immersed in a tattoo, everything around me fades out and time stands still. It's really hard to explain without it sounding trippy, but my mind engages with the piece and everything else seems irrelevant. I think this skill was honed from my years out on the streets. It was my escape from reality when times got tough out there. Don't get me wrong, my brain still functions with thought, but it's like it's on a separate path in my head and becomes a white noise.

Shannon turned out to be a rare perfect customer. The chat was minimal and she asked if I minded her putting headphones in to listen to her music. This is the best thing an artist can hear when undertaking a large tattoo that requires focus. The music relaxes her and I get to work in peace. We stop every hour for both of us to stretch out and take a drink. It is really important to take small breaks for the customer's sake but also for the artist. I have seen artists pound their client for six hours straight and by the end of it they are both beaten physically and mentally. Yes, tattoos hurt to get done, but it doesn't have to be a brutal experience.

As much as I was deep in my zone during this tattoo, I couldn't avoid the negative thoughts creeping in there, reminding me that my stalker was still at large. I wished I could just stay in the cocoon of safety here at the shop, but I know it's not an option.

"Okay girl, it looks like we are finished here. You sat really well for such a big piece. I am proud of you." As she sits up, the common look of relief is etched across her face.

"Thank you, it really wasn't as bad as I was expecting."

"That's good to hear, so if you would like to get up slowly and head on over to the mirror you can check out your new tattoo." This part is always an anxious moment for any artist. You have given it your best, but that still doesn't mean your client will be happy. Some have expectations beyond the realms of reality. There really is no such thing as a perfect tattoo. As she steps up to the mirror, I wait with bated breath for her reaction. She clasps her mouth with her shaking hand and begins to sob. Shit, this can go one of two ways.

"It's amazing, I absolutely love it." I am relieved to hear they are tears of happiness and not ones of 'What the fuck did you do to my leg?' I can't help but feel pride that she is so emotional over the piece I have just given her. I don't really like to study my own work as I always manage to find flaws, but as I clean it down for her one last time I am pretty happy with how this one turned out. My line work is solid and consistent and the color saturation seems to be sitting on the skin well. I know it must be good as I reach for my camera to take a picture for my portfolio. Not many make it in there; many fail the scrutiny test that I put them through. Shannon is excited that I am photographing her piece. I have to admit there has been many times when a client has asked if I would like to take a picture of the tattoo I had just done for them, and out of embarrassment I have taken one, knowing full well that it would never make it into my portfolio.

"Robyn is just going to love this. I can't wait for her to see it." Without having to ask, I know Robyn is her little girl. You can see the love in her eyes as she speaks her name. (I wonder if my mom ever had that look when she spoke about me?)

"Aww, I'm glad she will. You tell her I said hello and that her mommy was very brave getting this done." I wrap it up and run through the aftercare process making sure she understands the importance of it. So many good tattoos have been ruined due to improper aftercare. This can be the artist's fault for either not bothering to give any or telling them incorrect information. On the flip side it can be the customer's fault for either not bothering to follow the advice or using products they were advised not to. We sell all the proper aftercare for both tattoos and piercing and we try not to let any customer leave without buying it. Imagine spending hundreds of dollars on an amazing tattoo and then messing it all up by trying to save a couple of bucks on aftercare cream? It just doesn't make sense. Our customers actually get double aftercare speeches, one from their artist and then one from Zane, who pretty much insists you buy the proper stuff from us. It's nothing to do with profit, as the margin on these is very slim. It's making sure that they respect and look after the piece of art you have devoted your time and energy into to ensure it heals the best it can be. I hand Shannon her aftercare sheet and thank her once more for coming to see me.

"No, thank you, it was one of the best experiences of my life. Not to pry into your private life or anything, but I just wanted to say how brave you were handling that creep on the show last night. You are a fine example to every young girl out there. You stay strong." This was the first mention of last night's antics from her and it genuinely felt heartfelt. I wasn't annoyed by her words, which sort of surprised me.

"Thank you, that means a lot." It actually does mean a lot to hear those words of support right now. I begin to break down my station. My mind is back to full function and the worry comes flooding back in. After Zane is finished settling up with Shannon, he comes over to check that I am okay.

"Wow, Megan, that was a long session. How you feeling?"

"To be honest, it was a nice distraction to be back tattooing, but now that I am done I kind of feel like crap again."

"I hear you. Well, I am taking you to dinner when we finish up here and if you want, you can stay over at my place for as long as you like." I hate to be a burden on anyone, but for once my stubbornness doesn't get in the way.

"That would be great, thank you, Zane." It's a weight off my mind to have the offer of both company and a place to stay other than my apartment.

"Don't mention it; we can stop off on the way to get your things and pick up Jake."

"Oh yeah, I'm such a bad mom. I hadn't even thought about Jake. You sure you don't mind having him there?"

"Not at all, you know I love cats. He's just as welcome as you are. In fact, you may both end up staying there forever, one big happy family." He smiles his Cheshire grin and scurries off to continue his duties. I feel much better now knowing I didn't have to face tonight alone.

Normally I would go check out what tattoos the guys were doing when I had some free time, but today I find myself heading straight to the back room. As I close the door and cut out the shop floor noise, I take a moment to just breath. My moment is short lived as I spot the green glow from my cell illuminating from my handbag. I quickly retrieve it. 'Call from, Paul'. I was anxious to speak with him and I hit accept before it rings out.

"Hey Paul." He sounds surprised.

"Oh, hey Megan, I have been trying you all day."

"Yeah, sorry I'm at the shop. I was tattooing all day."

"You doin' alright?"

"As good as can be expected, I suppose." I have a small bit of venom in my words as I still feel anger towards him.

"Look, Megan, you have to believe me. I gave clear instructions that that topic was off limits. That's why we are looking into suing them. I have given them hell over it. They have promised a public apology, but I don't think that's such a good idea bringing it all up again on television. I know Detective Roberts is on the case, and I have given him as much information as possible to help him out." His breath sounds short and I'm quite sure he is eating a bagel as he speaks.

"Listen, I don't want to sue anybody, and I certainly don't want an apology. What happened is done. Maybe it will work out for the best. It has been going on for so long that maybe now it's time he was caught and I can go on living my life without the constant fear." I don't know where this sudden philosophical viewpoint has come from. If he had called me ten minutes ago when I was on the verge of another meltdown, I would have been calling for the television network's heads on a plate.

"You are right, Megan. It's time for all of this nonsense to stop. You know this guy Roberts seems to be the real deal, not like all those other wasters they assigned to you." My suspicions of bagel eating are confirmed as I have to hold the phone away from my ear to avoid hearing the loud chewing resonating from Paul's mouth.

"Well, hopefully he actually does something this time. He talks a good talk, I will give him that much."

"I hate to bring this up now, but I have to ask. What way do you want to handle the press? My phones have been ringing off the hook all day."

"I'm just not ready to talk to them yet. Give me a couple of days to get my head straight and then we can make a plan, okay?" As good as Paul is to me, I know this is every manager's golden ticket. Having the press at bidding wars as to who gets the exclusive story. He's also not stupid, and knows he has to play this one carefully with me or his job could be on the line.

"Of course, actually that's what I have already told them. When you are ready, we will pick the best possible option brought to the table. In the meantime, please don't speak with any reporters. You know how those vultures can twist your words." I refrain from bringing up the 'oh yes I know all about it, Paul, just like hosts on television shows asking questions they are not supposed to'. I simply leave it at, "I won't. I'll speak with you soon."

As I hang up my screen becomes filled with all of the missed calls and texts I missed during the day. I spend the next half an hour reading through them all. I am relieved to see there is no more contact from Sammy. My social media accounts are bursting with messages and comments of support, but again I feel I am not ready to post anything up just yet. Paul has always tried to convince me to employ someone to run my social media pages as many of the big 'celebrities' do these days, but I always argue. What's the point in having a page representing me but then having a stranger pretending to be me? It defeats the purpose, although sometimes I do wish I had listened to him as it's hard to keep up with it all.

As my head is buried in my phone, I hardly notice Zane has come in, and let a little jump when he speaks. "Sorry, Megan, Detective Roberts is here. He wants a word with you. I didn't mean to scare you."

"It's okay, I was a million miles away. Cool, send him in. Thanks babe." Roberts appears at the door looking somewhat fresher than this morning.

"Hi Megan, it's good to see you back at work; keep it normal."

"Yeah, it's helping keep my mind off things." He has a beige folder in his hands. I study it, curious of its content.

"So this may be nothing or it may be something. Do you know a Gary Feldman?" I run the name through my head trying to source a connection. Nothing clicks.

"No, I don't think so. The name doesn't seem familiar anyway." He looks a little disappointed, not the reaction he was hoping for. He opens the folder and hands me a photograph. It's a mug shot; the guy has a shaved head and a mean look in his eyes. I still don't make a connection, as much as I want to.

"You recognize him, Megan?" I look again but still nothing.

"No, I'm sorry, I don't."

"Okay, this is Gary Richard Feldman, convicted on charges of rape, abduction and robbery. He has served time in both Boston and New York, you tattooed this guy three years back, here in New York and his timeline follows yours almost exactly." Am I looking at the guy that has caused me all this misery? The fact that I tattooed him means I have had a blasé conversation with him while he plotted my demise. Could this really be him? He is not how I had pictured him in my mind. It's strange, I didn't have an exact vision of how he would look, but it just wasn't like this guy.

"I tattoo so many people, he just doesn't look familiar. Do you know what I tattooed on him?"
I realize how stupid the question sounds as I say it.

"No, we were actually hoping you would remember what it was. Lou gave us your client list and we crosschecked everybody on there and this guy is ringing alarm bells for us." I so badly wanted to remember him and give Roberts the ammunition he was seeking to nail this guy, but I had to be honest about it.

"So, did you arrest him then?" I say sounding more desperate than I intended.

"We have our best guys looking for him as we speak. We are very interested about what he has to say, Megan." I remain transfixed on the picture. Really? This guy, computer savvy and stealth like approach? This guy looked more like brute force and no patience. He just doesn't look right for a stalker. What is the right look for a stalker? I really don't think there is any answer to that question.

"If you think of anything, please call me. I will be sure to let you know as soon as we have spoken to him. Do you want me to send a guy over to see you home from here?"

"No, it's fine, thanks. I'm staying at Zane's tonight. If I remember anything, I will call you right away. I'm sorry I can't be of more help." He takes the photograph back fr om me and tidies it back into the folder.

"That's fine, Megan. It was a long time ago, but the brain is a funny thing. There might be some information locked away in there somewhere. If you find it, you know how to get me." Once again, he leaves me baffled by thought.

Zane reappears, "What was that all about? Did they find the guy?"

"They might have, and apparently I tattooed him a few years back, which makes me look like a fool. How could I not have spotted it?" Zane does his best to look shocked, but I can tell by his expression that he was eavesdropping in on our conversation.

"Don't be silly, Megan. How were you supposed to know that you were tattooing a deranged sociopath? Did they arrest him yet?"

"No, they are looking for him. How can I not remember him? The photo was a mean looking snarling guy. He's not someone you would easily forget. He said it looks like he followed me from Boston to here. I just don't know what to make of it all." I feel like crying again but tears don't come.

"Well, look, if this is the son of a bitch, then at least the cops are onto him. This is not your fault, Megan. Now, get your things. It's time we got out of here. I'm taking you to my favorite restaurant. With some food in your belly things will feel better, I promise." He leans in and gently kisses me on the forehead. I try to find the words without sounding corny.

"I am so lucky to have you; thank you for being here." He just smiles and whispers, "I wouldn't be anywhere else right now".

CHAPTER TEN

Bistro 76 is a quaint Italian style restaurant tucked away down a side street, away from the bustling streets of rushing footsteps and traffic. There are many restaurants like this scattered across Soho, but this is Zane's favorite. The dimly lit lighting and flickering candles add to the relaxed environment. Our table is at the back of the tiny restaurant and gives me a much needed sense of anonymity. The guys at the shop had offered to join us, but Zane was insistent that I needed some breathing space. He is probably right. We had slipped out the back of the shop, avoiding the awaiting photographers out front. Although there is no dress code, I do feel somewhat underdressed amongst the beautiful decor that surrounds us. Zane's good looks are amplified under the moody lighting.

"Isn't this place just gorgeous?"

"Yeah, it's so cute." I am suddenly self-aware that my response feels 'first date like'. It's funny when everyday situations with people are transported to a different venue, reactions and responses automatically change. I have never had feelings like that about Zane; he's like my brother and best friend all rolled into one. I shake it off and follow with a quick attempt at a joke to eradicate any hint of awkwardness, "Probably a bit too nice for the likes of us two." We both laugh and I am relieved to see he hasn't seemed to notice my over analysis.

The waiter approaches, decked out in a smart white shirt and neatly tied black bow tie. Gladly, he doesn't seem to have a clue who we are. Usually, you can tell by people's demeanor if they recognize you. They tend to overcompensate with niceness. This guy is friendly but relaxed.

"Hey guys, how are you this evening? Can I start you off with some drinks?" Before I have time to answer, Zane is already speaking, "We will have two very large mojitos to start with, and can you bring us a bottle of the house white wine please?" I know he is only trying to help, but I really can't help being irked by people who order for you. I don't bother correcting him with, *Actually, I want a beer, asshole!!!* Instead, I smile stupidly as if I am in on it. As our waiter heads off to retrieve our drinks, Zane is looking slightly smug,

"Trust me, after a few drinks things are going to seem a whole lot better." The voice inside my head answers, *I thought it was the food that was going to make me feel better, isn't that what he said earlier?* I shut the voice up with a shush, a little louder than I had planned. Zane notices and his smile fades, "Are you alright, Megan?"

"Yeah, sorry I'm just distracted." I raise my menu to shield my embarrassment as I pretend to read it. Perfect timing, as the waiter returns with our cocktails.

"Are you guys ready to order some food?" I give Zane a death stare. *Just you try and order for me again. I won't smile and nod this time.* He waits for me to speak and gestures his hand towards me. I panic order, as I hadn't really paid any attention to what was on there.

"Eh, I will have the vegetarian ravioli please." Even saying the words makes my stomach alert to the prospect of actually getting some food.

"Very good, and for you, sir?"

"I will have the lasagna with garlic bread."

"Excellent, I will return with your wine." He takes our menus and leaves us once again. This is strange; Zane and I always get on like a house on fire. Maybe the hunger is making me snappy. I have to keep reminding myself that he is just trying to help. I'm sure this situation is just as foreign to him as it is to me. I know I need to speak first to let him know that I am not angry with him.

"My God, I am starving. Thanks for taking me. I haven't eaten in like two days." He looks relieved as my words clear the awkward air.

"You have to eat, girl. Even if I have to force this down your throat, you have to eat up every bit." That's more like the Zane I know. I am lucky to have someone who worries about me as much as he does.

We sip our drinks while we wait for the arrival of our food. Before I know it, my glass is empty and the wine bottle is not far behind it. The alcohol goes straight to my head as there is no food blocking its path. I feel dizzy and giddy. The conversation flows between us and my subconscious is temporarily switched off. I hate admitting I was wrong, but Zane was right – I do feel a lot better with a few drinks down me. Our waiter is summoned numerous times over the next hour. We are slowly working our way through the cocktail menu. My words are becoming increasingly slurred each time we order. My cheeks are flushed from the alcohol thinning my blood. As another drink is placed down in front of me, I excuse myself and seek out the bathroom.

I try to compose my steps as I navigate through the tight setup of tables. I apologize as I bump into both people and their tables; my depth perception is clearly way off. I reach the bathroom with my dignity still somewhat intact. The bathroom is in keeping with the ambience of the restaurant. A silhouetted lady holding an umbrella is the sign on the door to indicate it is the ladies room. As you enter, metallic boudoir photo frames hang strategically on the walls. A large gold leaf mirror hangs from floor to ceiling and the sinks are stone basin. I don't have much time to admire its pleasant features, as I really need to pee now. I pick the nearest stall and hurriedly line the toilet seat with tissue paper. This is something I have done since I was a kid. I couldn't bear to be sitting on someone else's germs, but ironically I also do it at home as well, even though it's just me there. Instant relief flows through my body as I sit down and pee. All the alcohol from the last hour is leaving my body. When I am done, I use another piece of tissue to push the flusher and the same to open the locked door. I suppose I am a germaphobe, but I rarely notice my 'precaution' routines anymore.

While washing my hands, I examine myself in the mirror. I am far from looking my best, but the alcohol makes me not care and I don't bother trying to fix my smudged makeup. With a slightly clearer head, I make my way back out to the restaurant. A more confident stride now as I head back to our table. I notice Zane has his hand over my drink. He only notices my presence as I am a few feet away. Once he does he pulls his hand away fast and begins laughing. Confused, I ask him, "What were you doing to my drink, man?" He looks flustered.

"Oh, there was dirt or something on the rim. I know how particular you are, so I was trying to get it off before you came back, and now you probably won't want to drink it because my dirty fingers were on there." He is clearly drunk.

"It's okay, I know you're clean, Zane." We both giggle, but he's right. I would prefer a fresh drink.

I smell the food before I see it; the waiter places the steaming plate in front of me. I hope it was worth the hour wait, but at this stage I would eat it out of the dumpster if I had to. My stomach lets out a rumble that sounds like it's saying 'FEED ME'. I don't even wait for Zane's plate to be put down and I already have fork in hand and am shoveling the food into my mouth.

"Would you like any black pepper or parmesan cheese?" The waiter's question is just met with a shake of my head as my mouth is too full to speak. Zane looks at me with admiration.

"Jesus, slow down there, girl. Don't forget to chew." I just smile through my closed lips, frantically chewing to get it into my awaiting empty stomach. I demolish the dish in under five minutes, only stopping to take a sip of my wine to clear any food stuck in my throat. As I finish, I struggle for breath. An uncontrollable burp comes out and I try condense the noise as best as possible. Both of us burst out laughing.

"Such a lady," Zane says mockingly.

"I know, classy as always. My God, that was amazing." I sit back and let the food settle. They say it takes around ten minutes for your body to register the food. I will wait because right now I could eat that all over again. I take my cocktail and try to choose a part of the glass to drink from that looks the cleanest after Zane's fingers had been there. He continues to eat and I continue to drink.

"So, not to put a dampener on the evening, but have you heard anything from Roberts since earlier?" It has put a dampener on my good time; the food and drink have been masking the worry. Now at the mention of it the alcohol may accelerate my emotions.

"No, I haven't even checked my phone. I just hope they have picked that creep up." Sensing my tone, he apologizes for bringing it up. The conversation subsides as he finishes up his food. Our waiter comes to clear our dishes away.

"Can I interest you guys in any dessert?" I see this as my opportunity to get a little dig back at Zane from earlier.

"Yes, bring us four shots of Sambuca and two of your cheesecake slices, please." Zane just shrugs his shoulders and gives the waiter a knowing look. This time I smile smugly. I knock both shots back before I tuck into the light and fluffy cheesecake. My head is spinning once again, the concoction of food and alcohol spiking my blood sugar levels to exhilarating highs. We must have been here three hours now. With full bellies and clouded minds, it's time to get out of here. We settle the bill, which Zane insists on paying for. He leaves a generous tip for our waiter, whom we have kept busy since our arrival. I drunkenly thank him, and we head for the exit.

"Do you want to walk to my place? Some fresh air might do you good," Zane asks, as he has to hold my elbow to stop me nose diving down on to the floor. Normally, I can hold my drink quite well for a skinny ass girl, but I may have overdone it a bit this evening.

"Eh, I think a taxi is a better idea. My legs feel like jelly." He agrees and gets the girl on reception to call us one. We venture out into the cold to wait. The fresh air hits my flushed cheeks and immediately cools them down. It should come as no surprise, with my control freak tendencies, that I don't like feeling out of control. Right now, I don't feel like I have control over my bodily functions. I am holding on to Zane as he adjusts his stance to counterbalance my drunken sways.

"Don't worry, I've got you," he says trying to reassure me. Eventually the taxi pulls up and Zane escorts me into the back seat. I let the head rest take the weight of my body I have been struggling to hold up. As soon as my body relaxes, my eyes roll back into my head and I pass out. Caught somewhere in between consciousness and unconsciousness, somewhere close to dreams but stuck in reality. My body is shocked back awake as Zane shakes me by the shoulder.

"Wake up sleepy head. We are here, and this man needs his taxi back." I open my eyes hard to fight off the drowsiness.

"Sorry, I must have drifted off," I respond with slurred speech, my body still rattling with adrenaline after the shock of been awoken so abruptly. Zane lives on the East side. The buildings here are a lot older. His apartment block is an old yarn factory that has been converted. The original dirty red brick remains and a large round chimney pokes out of the square roof. Zane comes around and opens my door. He helps me get to my feet, which still feel heavy. We slowly walk to the main door. There is no fancy security door man here, just a keypad on the wall requiring an access pass code. The door buzzes open as he punches in the code. The elevators are the old school kind that you have to pull the rail guard open to gain access. The words 'old' and 'elevator' should not be used in the same sentence in my opinion, but I am in no fit state to complain, and I clamor in. I lean against the wall as it takes us up floor by floor; creaks and moans ring out as it does so.

"I think we may have overdone it on the cocktails," Zane says, but is clearly not in half the state I am.

"Yeah, I'm wasted man," are the only words I can get out. The elevator grinds to a halt and the doors open. I could never live in an apartment like this because the doors open right into your apartment. So, if someone hits the wrong floor they can easily end up looking straight into your home. You have to wonder if places like this are still legal – surely it's a huge security risk. When I mumble a short rant about it to Zane, he reassures me that once you are inside you can put a block on it opening at your door. My drunken mind is clearly not up for an intellectual conversation as I respond with, "It's just fucking weird, man."

The apartment is simplistic. Exposed brick is left in places, giving it a rustic but cold feeling. A beautiful open fireplace sits in the center of the room, a feature that probably adds thousands on to the price tag but is certainly worth every cent. A large plasma TV hangs mounted on the wall above it, kind of ruining the feature of the intricate stone work. I plonk myself down on to the leather couch.

"Do you want a drink or anything?" I couldn't bear to drink any more alcohol.

"Just some water, please." Zane goes to the kitchen and retrieves me an ice cold bottle of water from the fridge. I am dehydrated but also still full from the dinner, so I just take baby sips.

"I'm sorry, but I think I need to get to my bed." I can feel my eyes starting to shut down again and I want to make the move before I pass out on the couch.

"No problem, the spare room should be all set up." I force my body off the couch and get to my feet. Then Zane shouts out a loud "Shit".

I try to focus and ask, "What's wrong?"

He holds his face with one hand. "We totally forgot about Jake." I feel immediate guilt that I never even gave it a second thought, or a first thought for that matter.

"Oh my God, I can't believe I forgot. My head's all over the place."

"It's okay, don't blame yourself. Listen, give me your keys and I will get a cab over there to get him. I can pick up your toothbrush and some clothes too." My mind struggles with the simple information presented. Normally, I would argue about not putting him out and offer to go do it myself, but I just reply with, "You are so good, thank you." I shuffle down the hallway to the spare room following Zane.

"You get into bed, and I will be as quick as I can. Where are your keys?" I climb under the covers and for the second night in a row don't bother to remove my clothes.

"They are in my handbag. Make sure to grab Jake's food and litter tray."

"Okay, you just relax. I will be back soon."

Just as my eyes begin to drift off, I call for Zane as he is closing over my door, "Zane?"

"Yes?"

"Please make sure the elevator door is locked." Before I hear any reply, I am gone, back in the grip of unconsciousness.

I pry my eyes open, breaking the crust that has formed during my slumber. My body still feels heavy as I try to move from my side onto my back. I feel cold and disorientated. I have no idea how long I have been asleep, but from the darkness of my room I can only presume it is still in the depths of nighttime. Pulling my body up onto the pillow, I struggle as I heave myself upright. I wonder if Zane is back yet? In the darkness I strain my ears to try to hear any commotion coming from the kitchen, but the only thing I can hear is my imagination running riot. What if my stalker has murdered Zane on his way to my apartment and now he is here to get me? My palms begin to sweat at this notion, but the rest of my body remains cold. My eyes are beginning to adjust to the darkness and I can now make out shapes around me. Just as I am about to get up to investigate, my heart stops dead as the door shifts through the blackness.

I blink hard to make sure it is not just my paranoia. I'm sure I noticed the tiniest movement from the corner of my eye. I stare hard through the darkness and wait for it to happen again. Just as I begin to blame it on my mind playing tricks, it moves again. Little by little, it silently opens wider but I can't see any figure. I whisper "Who's there?"

Ironically it's something I always complain about in horror movies, as surely it is better to remain silent if a homicidal maniac is searching for you in darkness, but now I am in this situation it seems a natural instinct to request identification. I grip the duvet cover as hard as possible. I know there is someone in the room. I can't see them, but I can feel their presence. Slowly, I slide my legs away from the side of the bed – the fear of them being grabbed and then dragged to my impending doom is all too real. Suddenly, a sound cuts through the silence, "Meow." I feel instant relief as I realize it is just my cat, Jake, but still jump as he hops up onto the bed.

"You just gave Mommy a heart attack." His black fur is still invisible in the darkness, but his yellow eyes shine bright. He nuzzles up to my chin and I return the affection by scratching his head. I am glad it is just his whiskers stabbing me and not a knife wielding psychopath. I'm not sure how much more of this stress my body can take. Now that I have confirmation that Zane has returned, I need to go and make sure everything is okay. It takes all of my effort to slide my body out of the bed. My legs feel like lead weights as I stand up. I hate being in a strange room where I have no idea where the light switch is located. It makes you feel helpless, especially in situations like what has just happened. Normally, I would always make a checklist before going to sleep in a strange place, but I was in no fit state to last night.

I shuffle across the wooden floor with my arm outstretched, waiting to make contact with the adjacent wall. I can only assume that logically the light switch should be beside the door. I slide my hand along the cold wall and find the switch – success. Waiting for the relief of illumination, I push down. It makes a click, but there is no light. I try again but nothing happens. This night is testing all of my worst fears. Peering out into the dark hallway, I wait to see a face looking back at me. My body shakes, a mixture of being terrified and also being freezing cold. I have no choice but to continue out into the hallway. I raise my arms out in front of my face, fists clenched, and tentatively make my way down the long corridor. The kitchen in front of me remains in darkness. As I reach the end, I lean against the corner wall and slowly push my head forward to try to get a view into the living room area. I push my head far enough for one eye to get a view.

To my surprise, there is a blue light glowing from the far end of the room. It takes me a second to realize the light is radiating from an open laptop sitting on the table up on the high rise of the apartment floor. As my vision focuses, I can now see there is a silhouette of a person sitting behind the table. I strain harder to see if I can make out their face, but my legs are distracted and I lose my balance. Stumbling forward, my left foot makes a loud thud against the wooden floorboards. The silhouetted figure's head shoots up to stare right at me, then the laptop slams down hard. Darkness, complete darkness. Silence, deafening silence. We each wait for the other to speak. I contemplate making a bolt for the elevator, but with my lethargic body I don't fancy my chances.

"Megan." The silence is broken. It sounds like Zane, but I have to make sure.

"Zane, is that you?"

"Yeah, it's me. Hold on, I have a flashlight here." The room bursts into light as the flashlight is switched on. My body unclenches as I can now see Zane clearly.

"Jesus, I thought you were asleep. You frightened me. Are you okay? You look awful." He walks towards me, the beams of light blinding my sight as he approaches.

"Well, I was, but I woke up and wanted to check you were back okay. Jake nearly gave me a heart attack coming into my room, and then my light wouldn't switch on. I was freaking out, man." "Yeah, the power is out. In this old building, the circuit breakers are always giving up. I got back with Jake a while ago, but I just thought I'd let you sleep. You were pretty wasted last night."

"Yeah, I feel like crap. Those cocktails must have been pretty strong. What were you doing on the laptop?"

"Oh, just catching up on some work stuff. Here, you are shaking. Let me make you a cup of tea."

I give him a look with my eyebrow raised, "And how are you going to do that with no electricity, Einstein?" As it dawns on him, we both giggle. He picks up a throw from the couch and wraps it around my shoulders.

"C'mon, we will get you back to bed. I have some candles I can light for you."

"That would be good, thanks. I just want to check my phone. Hold on." I pick up my bag off the kitchen counter and look for my phone. Unsuccessful, I bring it over towards Zane's flashlight. It's not there.

"Have you seen it anywhere?"

"No, I hope you didn't lose it in the taxi."

"Shit, that's all I need." Dismayed, I turn to head back to the bedroom, but just as I do I notice a glowing light coming from the laptop table.

"Hey, is that your phone over there?" Zane stops and shines the flashlight back at me.

"Eh, no I have my phone here." I walk across the room and sure enough, there is my phone sitting right beside the laptop. The screen is glowing with message and email notifications. As I walk back towards Zane, I can't help but be confused. "I thought you said you hadn't seen my phone?" I sound accusing.

"I didn't even notice it there. I mean it is pretty dark in here. You must have put it down in your drunken state." As out of it as I was, I was pretty sure I was nowhere near that part of the room. I follow Zane back down the hallway and don't bother to push the matter any further. I'm just glad that I hadn't lost it in the taxi.

Zane ducks into the bathroom to grab some candles and I take the opportunity to check my messages. I click into my inbox and scroll down through the numerous texts. As I get to the top, my pulse raises, as yet again there is the sight of Sammy's name staring back at me. 'Message sent at 2:42am' It's now just past 3am.

"Zane, I got another one."

He emerges from the bathroom with a confused look. "Got another what?" I hold out the phone for him to see.

"Text message from Sammy."

"Shit, have you opened it yet?"

"No, will you do it for me?"

He clicks on it and silently reads it to himself. "Do you want to know what it says?" I nod my head to proceed.

"Dear Megan, I have watched you from afar for so long. Now I have you close to me, I can protect you. I will never let them harm you. I have seen their evil. I am your guardian angel. Soon you will realize this."

Zane waits for my reaction. "This is messed up, like, this guy sounds deranged on a whole other level, man. What does he mean he now has me close? I think he's going to try snatch me." Zane looks angry.

"You know what? At least he is saying that he is going to try protect you. He doesn't want to hurt you, Megan. That's gotta count for something, right?" I am a bit surprised by his reaction; normally Zane is so chilled out and understanding. It's rare to see him snap like that. Maybe he is just losing patience with me and the whole fucked up situation. I choose my next words carefully.

"I suppose so, but c'mon this nut job is texting me from our dead best friend's phone, and even if he doesn't want to hurt me, it still sounds like he wants me as his prisoner."

He sounds more sympathetic this time, "I know it's hard, but don't worry. I will look after you." He places his arm around my shoulder and begins to walk me back to the bedroom. He lights some candles and places them around the room. Shadows dance across the wall against the flickering light. Jake is curled up fast asleep on my pillow.

"Was everything okay when you went over to my apartment?"

"Oh yeah, everything was fine. I put together a bag of clothes for you and turned your heating off."

"You are a star, thank you so much. I'm sorry for being a pain in the ass. Was Spike okay about letting you in?"

"Yep, I just explained the situation to him, and don't worry – I'm used to you being a pain in my Ass." He smiles and kisses my forehead. "Now you try and relax. I am right down the hall if you need me." I really don't want him to leave me alone, but reluctantly I let him walk out leaving me with my snoring cat. My mind tick tocks back and forth with thoughts. I play out kidnapping scenarios to their full conclusion, which always ends with my death. No matter how hard I try to think about another subject matter, the negative thoughts creep their way back in. As my tired mind repeatedly attempts to fall asleep, it is repeatedly awoken by my body jumping it back awake. Eventually my body stays still just long enough to drift off into a broken sleep.

"Morning sleepy head, wakey, wakey." As I open my eyes, I see Zane standing there with a plate of sizzling food. I have never been so glad to see the morning sunshine after that turbulent night. "Breakfast is served," he says in his best attempt at an English accent. He places it down on the dresser beside me.

"Wow, that looks amazing."

"Would you like tea or coffee, madam?" keeping up the pantomime of an English butler.

"Coffee would be divine, darling," I say in my best posh English accent to go along with it. I am surprisingly hungry again after stuffing my face at the restaurant last night. I really cannot remember the last time

I had breakfast in bed. I tuck into my eggs benedict as Zane returns whistling up the hall with my coffee.

"My, you are in good form this morning."

"The morning is the best part of the day. A good breakfast is always the right start. Once you are living under my roof, you shall be treated like a princess." I can't help but smile as he dances around the room laying out fresh towels for me and opening up the curtains. I am usually not good in the mornings. No human contact for at least an hour when woken up, that's the usual rule, but after the trauma of last night, Zane's comic relief is most welcome.

"So the electricity is back then?" I ask, interrupting his no song in particular whistling.

"Yeah, I went down there myself this morning and changed the fuse. You would be all day waiting for maintenance to do it; they are useless."

"These eggs are to die for. How are you single?"

"I know, that's what I keep telling everyone." He laughs at his own joke, but I can tell he is pleased with the compliment. For as long as I have known Zane, I have always had my suspicions as to whether he was gay or not. I mean, he has had a few girlfriends over the years, but all were short lived. He is quite camp in his nature but tends to man it up a bit when he's at the shop surrounded by testosterone filled guys. I have never questioned him about it, but would like to think as one of his best friends that he could confide in me if he wanted to.

"Okay, so there are fresh towels there if you want to take a shower. I left your wash bag and clothes in the bathroom. Don't kill me if I didn't pick you out the right clothes. I was pretty drunk."

"I'm sure they are fine, thank you. What time are you heading into the shop today?" Now Zane returns the look I gave him about the kettle last night.

"Today is Sunday, you mad woman. Jesus, you really must be losing your mind. Today, we can do whatever you want to do." He was right. I had no idea what day it was, and he is probably also right about me losing my mind.

I head to the bathroom for my shower. My clothes are neatly arranged in a pile. He mustn't have been that drunk as they are fully coordinated from socks to underwear. His ability to color coordinate clothes only adds to my doubts about his sexuality. I'm not one to stereotype, but 90% of straight men have no clue how to dress properly, and Zane is always superbly decked out in designer clothing.
After a long shower I brush my teeth and do my hair. The hangover is still lingering, but I feel a hell of a lot better.

I throw my bags into the bedroom. Zane has neatly made my bed and cleared the dishes. He really is looking after me well. Soft jazz music is coming from the living room. I walk down the same corridor that terrified me in the dark last night. It now seems silly how scared I was. Zane is cleaning the pots up from breakfast and is swaying to the beat of the music as he does so. I stand and watch him for a moment.

"Nice moves, man." He jumps with fright and drops the pan in his hand.

"Jesus, how long you been standing there? You scared me half to death." I shouldn't laugh as I know the feeling, but I can't help it. "Was the shower okay?"

"Yeah, it was perfect, and thanks for the clothes. You want some help cleaning up?"

"Nah, I got it. You go chill out on the couch."

"Oh, do you have my phone?" Only now I remembered that I never took it back off him after he read the creepy text to me.

"Oh yeah, it's over there on the table." I am ready to catch up on my emails as my head feels in a better place. I pick it up and sit down on the couch, but as I press the buttons it is clear that the battery is dead.

"Shit, my cell is dead. Do you have a charger?"

"No, sorry honey, my phone is not the same as yours. I should have picked it up for you last night, but I never even thought of it."

"Ah, it's not your fault. I can swing by later and get it." I knew Roberts would be looking for me and Paul is probably pulling his hair out dealing with everything.

"Maybe it's best to just leave it off. I mean, that guy obviously has your number and it might be best to just lay low. Even being out in public might not be good for you right now." I suddenly feel very claustrophobic by his words. I hate anyone telling me what I can and can't do, but especially when it comes to my independence.

"I'm not going to lock myself away because of this guy" My reply is one of conviction and defiance. Zane walks over to me.

"I know. I'm not saying forever, but maybe just until things cool off a bit." I am trying not to overreact, but I don't even like feeling that I should be hiding away or that he feels I should be. My breathing gets shallow as I feel the walls closing in around me. I take a deep breath.

"I know you are only trying to help, but it's freaking me out. I have to speak to Roberts and find out if they caught that guy, and I told Paul I would check in with him." As I talk, I find myself rising from the couch and walking towards the elevator. I need to get out of here. Zane stands in my way and as I try to walk past him, he grabs me tight by the shoulders.

"Megan, calm down. You are getting worked up over nothing. Forget about what I just said. I'm just looking out for you. Breath. That's it, just calm down, come and sit down." I find myself being led back to the couch, even though it's not what I want. I know I overreacted, but I was shocked by both Zane's words and his actions. He continues words of calming and explaining himself, but his words are a blur. My mind has now reached a dark place, a conclusion that for the first time leads to suspicion. He couldn't be the one, could he? Out of all the people I had suspected over the years, Zane was never even in the equation.

As he speaks, I start putting pieces together to see if they fit. The timelines and locations match up, but so do many others that I know. He has always been very protective over me, but that's what friends do. Although he wasn't a tattoo artist, he still painted as a hobby – that would explain the crude artwork left for me. He was skilled on computers – he had to be as manager of the shop. I have ran through this checklist so many times over the years, I know how easy it is to link everything together when you are looking for an answer that sometimes isn't there. But what if? What if I had been this blind for all these years?

This guy kneeling in front of me, my best friend, a guy I worked with every day, could he be responsible for all the torment I have endured? And if it is him, he now has me. That's why he didn't want me to leave and why my phone is conveniently dead.

As he finishes speaking and awaits my reply, I look at him in a completely different light. Was his charming demeanor all an act? Behind that smile was there a psychopath lurking? I have no idea what he had just said, but I know I need to reply with something quick.

"Maybe you are right. Sorry I got so worked up. I'm just all over the place at the moment." I can see it's what he wanted to hear and there's that smile again. A smile I was seeing past for the first time.

"Okay, I'm going to make us some herbal tea." As he heads off to the kitchen, I begin to plan an escape if it comes to it. The freshly washed pans would make a sturdy weapon or the selection of knives that hung up around the cooker might be more effective. I can't believe I am thinking like this about the one guy who was closest to me in the world. His insistence on joining him for dinner was fitting in with the pieces of the quickly forming jigsaw. My eggs benedict churns in my stomach. Then, another horrible thought hits me like a brick to the face. Did he drug me? Was that the reason I was so out of it and passed out? His hand over my drink when I returned from the bathroom, stirring the powder with his finger to hide the evidence. If I was drugged, what happened while I was passed out? Did he cut the electricity to work in the shadows?

So many questions are burning inside me, but I daren't ask any as this could well be my stalker making me a cup of fucking herbal tea. Jesus

Christ, what was he doing on that laptop when I disturbed him? That text message was sent just minutes before I came down. Slowly, I was convincing myself that it had to be him. But why? We were already close from the very start and there was never any hint of chemistry between us. I suppose now that I think about it, he was never a fan of any of my boyfriends and always seemed to find fault with them, even Billy, whom he was friends with. He returns with our tea and interrupts my train of thought. He sits on the coffee table opposite me.

"You feeling a bit better now?" *Get the hell out of here, Megan. This guy is going to cut you up and bathe in your blood!* my subconscious screams at me from the inside, but I have to play this smart.

"Yeah, much better now." I try to act as cool as possible. I don't want to trigger a reaction from him.

"You know what might cheer you up? I have loads of art supplies in the spare room. I could set you up an easel over there by the window and you can paint all day if you like."

"That sounds great. Actually, I'd like to do that now, if you don't mind."

He looks at me suspicious, "If you don't mind? Not like you to be so mannerly, Megan. What's up?" My attempt at playing it cool had backfired. He was right. My normal tone was sarcastic and witty.

"Oh, I'm just trying to be nice because you are looking after me so well." He doesn't look convinced and heads off to the spare bedroom. Of course this is what I wanted. As soon as he is out of sight, I silently leap up off the couch and get to the elevator door as fast as possible. I hit the button, but a red circle appears with the word 'LOCKED' across it. A word that could seal my fate in this square box of bricks. I try the button once more before I retreat to the couch. I need to find that code. Just as my ass hits the seat, Zane returns. I try and hold my exasperated breath. He glances at the elevator door and then back to me. My only route out of here is locked, and he knows it. He continues to set up my art corner and I pretend to be interested, but really my mind is working on an escape plan. As I sit down in front of the blank canvas, it is the first time in my life that I don't actually want to paint anything. Zane stands beside me waiting for the brush to hit the canvas, but I don't move.

"Something wrong, Megan?"

"Um, I can't paint with you watching me."

"Oh, okay then, an artist needs their space, eh?" He walks away but only as far as the kitchen. I was getting to the stage of thought that the only way I was getting out of here alive was to inflict injury to him before he did it to me. I pretend to start painting, but really I just aimlessly swirl some black paint around the canvas. I keep checking over my shoulder to make sure he hasn't snuck up on me. I have visions of a knife being plunged into my back repeatedly. As my delusions accelerate, my hope diminishes.

An hour passes; I am deep in thoughts of escape, but then a sound cuts through the smooth jazz music that has remained playing – the sound is a buzzer. At first, I think it is a timer from the kitchen, but as it rings again I realize it is from the intercom system. I try to not look too excited as I turn around to face Zane to see if he is going to respond. He lets it ring again and then slowly moves towards the mesh panel on the wall. As he pushes down the button, I sit forward in anticipation of who it could be.

"Hello," a crackling sound comes through, but no voice. Silently, I urge him to try it again. The buzzer sounds again, "Hello," and then a voice breaks through the distortion.

"Hi, this is Detective Roberts with the NYPD." I close my eyes with relief. He knew I was here the relief I feel as I now remember telling him at the shop yesterday. This man may have just saved my life because he is good at his job.

"Oh, hi detective, come on up." He pushes the button down without putting up a fight. He must know there is no way out. He turns to me, "Your Detective is here. I didn't even know he knew you were here." I feel he is testing me.

"No, neither did I." He punches in a code on the elevator keypad and the red light turns to green. The doors open. I am ecstatic to see Roberts' lanky frame emerge into the apartment but don't let my emotions show. Now I need to just make sure that I leave with him without revealing Zane's true identity. I'm not sure if Roberts even carried a gun, his body always covered by his large trench coat. Zane approaches Roberts with an outstretched hand and shakes it strongly. I stand up and slowly make my way towards him. I hope that his years doing this job can tell by my expression that I needed help.

"Megan, I was trying your cell. You had me worried."

"Yeah, sorry, my battery is dead and Zane offered me a bed here so I wasn't alone." I wait for Zane to look away at any point to let Roberts know he had to get me out of here, but he never breaks his gaze.

"Dont worry, I have been looking after her." Roberts look unimpressed at Zane's attempt at charm.

"Okay, just in the future check in with me to let know you are alright. Now, I have some news about our suspect. We picked him up last night, but it seems he's not our guy. His alibi checks out and after talking with him at length he just doesn't fit the profile." I could have told you that just by looking at the picture, but now is not the time to be smug.

"So, you have no leads then?" Zane asks trying to sound concerned. Please see through the charade, Roberts.

"We are looking at different angles now. Sometimes it's not always about who and more about what. How you holding up, Megan?" Now is my chance to make a move.

"Yeah, I'm fine. Zane has been great. Eh, you know those files you were showing me yesterday? Well, I'd really like to take another look. I have been thinking about it and I may have remembered some stuff now that my mind is a bit clearer." Roberts looks a bit surprised at my statement.

"Okay, good, I don't have them here with me, though."

Zane chips in, "I can bring Megan down to the station later if you want, Detective." Before he has time to answer, I speak first.

"I'd like to go there now with you while it is still fresh in my mind, if that's okay." I am desperately trying to not sound desperate, but I am not so sure how well I am hiding it. I know if Roberts leaves here without me, I am never getting out of here. Finally, I think he has sensed something is not quite right here.

"Sure, that's no problem. My car is just outside. We can go there right now." Zane doesn't appear to react to the news. I suppose that's a sign of a sociopath, controlling their emotions on the outside but volcanoes are erupting deep inside.

"Perfect, I just need to grab something from the bedroom." I walk fast down the hallway and into the bedroom. I slip on my shoes, grab my bag and then frantically search for Jake. He's not here. I can't leave without him. I check the spare bedroom and then Zane's room, but there is no sign of him. I don't want to raise suspicions by telling Roberts I can't leave without him. Then, to my delight, Jake appears out from the bathroom door, his nose and whiskers wet from drinking out of the tap.

"There you are, baby." I pick him up and gently place him inside my bag. I return to the living room; you could cut the atmosphere with a knife.

"You are taking your bag? Do you want me to come with you?" Zane asks as a last ditch attempt to maintain his facade.

"No, that's okay. I will be back shortly." With that, he gives me a hug and whispers in my ear, "I will be here waiting for you." I don't respond to his chilling words and head straight for the open doors of the elevator. As the doors close, I breathe another sigh of relief. We don't speak any words on our descent. I am saving it for the car. We reach the bottom and make our way towards the exit. The stench of mold from the damp, old walls is overpowering. I didn't even notice it last night. As the doors are pushed open and the fresh air hits my face, I know I am lucky to have escaped the clutches of my tormenter.

Diary Entry

I felt nothing.

Now that I have written it on this page it sounds so cold, almost devoid of emotion. From an outside perspective it could be deemed as callous. I wanted to write it down because every time I try to make sense of it in my head, it gets clouded and consumed by excuses. What I felt that day was a feeling of nothing. I knew I should have felt something, or at least acted like I felt something. Years of numbness created to block out the pain had stayed with me right up until that day. My brother was really the only one who understood, but he avoided my eye contact. Stepfathers and boyfriends were nowhere to be seen. Even at my young age there was no sadness, no tears, no empathy. Words spoken with no real conviction or knowing, rhymed off in a set order of habit. Empty seats and empty words. I can remember being distracted by the paintings. The depictions of betrayal resonated with me the most that day. There are many forms of betrayal, but to betray your own child is unforgivable. I did feel something, if I am to be honest, but what I felt was wrong. I am ashamed to admit it, but I felt relief. The burden had been lifted, but ironically it was being lowered into the ground. Am I a bad person? Only someone with selfish tendencies could think this way at a time like this. I was eight years old and had been through far too much than any child should have, but does this justify feeling relieved that my mother was dead?

I ignored the cucumber sandwiches and the priest's empty words. I waited outside on the steps to be brought to my new family. For the first time in my young life, I felt hope, a guilt-ridden hope.

CHAPTER ELEVEN

I have so much information waiting to pour out that I don't know where to even start. Roberts' car suits his persona, battered and worn out. Just as the miles on the clock have taken their toll on the engine, the same applies to Roberts' body, from the years he has so obviously given to the job. It's a strange one-way relationship. He knows everything about me and I know absolutely nothing about him. Right now, he is my savior and I don't think he quite realizes it yet. I open up my bag to make sure Jake is okay. He actually looks quite cozy nesting amongst my clothes.

Roberts looks over, "Is that a cat?" I just smile as his question really doesn't require an answer. I wait until the engine has chugged into life before I speak. "Okay, just get out of here. I need to speak with you." He takes turns between looking at the road and back to me as he makes a wide U-turn.

"What is it, Megan? Is that why you were acting so strange in there?"

I really don't know where to begin until the words come out, "It's him, it's fucking him." Now I am away from the tension of being confined to Zane's presence, I am even more disgusted at the realization that he has done this to me. Roberts looks surprised by my revelation but remains reserved as per usual.

"You mean Zane? Right, tell me everything." I then explode into the whole frantic explanation that has been dying to get out. I tell him about the restaurant and the fact I think that he drugged me, about the laptop, and the text message from Sammy. I flip backwards to fill in the gaps about how he was so protective over me and hated my boyfriends. I tell him how he didn't want me to leave his apartment and if it wasn't for him, I don't like to think what would have happened. Roberts just listens without interruption. My timeline scale jumps back and forth as I try to convince him that it all makes sense. I must have been talking for ten minutes straight. When I take a moment for a breath, Roberts can finally get a chance to speak.

"Listen, we need to get you into the station and get this all written down. If he is the guy, then he is obviously really clever and we have to do this one smart. By the way, did you go back to your apartment at all after work last night?" I can't believe I left that part out during my ten-minute outburst.

"No, we had planned to go pick up Jake after the restaurant." This time he does interrupt me.

"And who is Jake?"

"Oh, Jake is this guy." I point down at Jake, who is now fast asleep and purring loudly. Roberts nods his head knowingly.

"So yeah, we had planned on going over there, but then I got so out of it that I completely forgot. Just as I was heading to bed at Zane's, he suddenly remembered and offered to go over there and get him. I gave him my keys and then I passed out."

"And what time was this at?"

I think hard. "I honestly have no clue. I was just trying to keep my eyes open at that stage."

"Do you have any idea how long he was gone for?"

"No, but when I woke up he was already back. That's when I disturbed him at his laptop in the dark. It was around 2:40 am because I checked my phone soon after."

"Did you notice anything strange about Zane's appearance or his clothing?" His line of questioning was beginning to throw me.

"Not that I noticed, why?" I can see his facial expression is now strained.

"Look, I have to tell you something, but I don't want you to freak out, okay?" Jesus, what now?

"Okay, I won't." This is a common lie told by people when they want to hear what you have to say and then they react to the information accordingly anyway.

"Your building's doorman, Spike, was found murdered last night." He waits for my reaction, but I just sit there staring at the dashboard. I try to make sense of it before I speak. I only come to one conclusion – Spike's death is my fault.

"And you think Zane did it?" It's the only question I want to know the answer to.

"Well, look, this information about Zane is obviously new to me. He wasn't on our list of suspects until now. It's something we are going to have to look into." My life is spiraling out of control at an ever increasing pace. Who am I to cause a poor innocent man's death?

"Poor Spike, he was the loveliest man you could ever meet. How did it happen?" A question I didn't really want the answer to, but I couldn't help asking it anyway.

"He was found in a dumpster strangled this morning behind your apartment block. This may just be a coincidence and might have nothing to do with your case." The information makes me want to puke. I can't get the image of his face struggling for breath out of my mind. Of course it wasn't a coincidence. When I add Zane into that scenario as the perpetrator, it makes my spine chill.

"But why?" I am searching for validation to rid me of this guilt I feel.

"It's too early to say, I'm afraid. The autopsy results will be back later and should tell us more. We do know that neither his wallet or watch were taken, so this suggests premeditation and not just a random mugging gone wrong." I spend the rest of the car journey sitting in silence. My brain searches for any justification for Spike's death, but there is none to be found.

Cop stations have always made me anxious, but today as we pull up outside I can't think of anywhere else I'd rather be. As we pass cops on the way in, I can't help feeling their judging eyes on me. I want to scream my innocence as a victim and not a perp. I'm not quite sure why it bothers me, but it does. Jake pops his head out of my bag as we walk to see what's going on. I try and gently hide him by coaxing his head back down. As we approach the main booking desk, Roberts instructs me to take a seat while he goes and speaks with the Police Chief. I sit on the hard plastic chair and watch as the hectic station goes about its daily routine. Cops come and go at a regular pace, some bring handcuffed criminals with them and others just bring coffee. There is bravado amongst the cops, much to the disdain of the arrested waiting to be booked in. After a short amount of time Roberts comes to get me.

"Okay Megan, we are having Zane picked up right now. I want you to come back with me and we can get a statement. Officer Briggs here is going to take Jake down to our private quarters. Don't worry, you are safe here." The more I hear that sentence, the less I believe it. I don't like handing Jake over to a stranger, even if they are wearing a uniform. Gently, I kiss his head to let him know that everything's okay. 'What the hell is going on?' is the look he gives me back. I follow Roberts up the stairs and into interview room 3. There is already a uniformed cop waiting for us. He nods his head as we enter. Roberts gestures to the seat for me to sit down.

"Would you like a coffee or a water?"

"A coffee would be great, thanks." Roberts just throws a look at the standing cop and without a word spoken, he walks out of the room to go retrieve my coffee. I know the cops work in ranks just like the army, but it still must feel pretty demeaning to be the coffee errand boy.

"Okay, I am going to turn on this tape recorder when you are ready. Just take it nice and slow. There is no rush here. The more information you can tell us, the better. No matter how small the detail is, I want you to say it. You never know what other information it can trigger."

The disgruntled cop returns and places my cup of coffee down in front of me. "Thank you." He doesn't reply and resumes his standing position against the wall. *Obviously speaking is not included in his pay packet*, I think to myself as I take a sip of the lukewarm, bitter coffee.

"Are you ready?" Roberts hits the record button. I spend the next hour repeating my story, trying to remember every detail. The more I speak, the more the dots connect. I remember silly things Zane said which seemed harmless at the time, but now when I put them all together they have a hidden venom behind them. Roberts doesn't have to ask many questions as I talk at length after each one. I can't believe how stupid I was to not have seen what was right in front of me. After some time, Roberts looks at his watch.

"Okay Megan, we are nearly done. Just one last question, when you were on the *Michael Corbett Show*, you had a phone call from a person that we believe to be your stalker. This was live on air. Did that person sound like Zane Norton?" I hadn't even thought about that. In some way my brain hadn't even made the link that this was the same person. I think for a moment.

"Well, no, not really, but it was quite muffled, so I don't really know."

"Alright, so you couldn't identify the voice as Zane Norton for sure? He was also with the guys you work with at the tattoo shop, live on a video link, moments before the phone call, correct?" If I thought I couldn't have felt any more stupid today, I was wrong. Now I am questioning everything again. How could it have been Zane making the call if he was with the guys? I stumble to get to an answer. "No, I couldn't be sure about the voice. It all happened so fast. Maybe if I could hear it again I might be able to tell better, and, yes, he was with the guys on the video link, but maybe he snuck away to make the call after it. Do you think it wasn't him?" I know it's not the normal approach of a police interview to revert the question back to them, but I really wanted to know what Roberts thought. His last questions seemed to be doubting my whole accusation now and I felt confused.

"Do you think it was him?" he asks as a response to my question. His tone is impatient for the first time. All I can offer him is a meek look in my eyes and a somber reply of, "I really don't know."
With that he stops the tape recorder.

"Look Megan, I know that was hard, but I have to ask these questions. If we don't have any concrete evidence, then we really don't have a case. We have no eyewitnesses or any fingerprints to match from the crime scenes. At the moment all we have is conjecture. If we could match the voice on the phone that night to Zane, then it might be our only avenue, but we have looked into it and we believe some form of device was used to distort and disguise his voice. We have your statement that he left his apartment last night to go to your apartment, but unfortunately you don't have a specific timeline. The perpetrator of Spike's murder was very careful not to be picked up on any security cameras and obviously knew the area well enough to avoid detection. We are waiting on forensics to see if any fingerprints or evidence were left at the scene, but really we aren't holding our breath for any to show up. The fact of the matter is if it is Zane, we might not actually have enough evidence to prosecute him and he may walk free. This is something you really have to prepare for, because at the moment it's just his word against yours. We want to run a test on you to see if there are any drugs in your system that he may have slipped into your drink. I am personally going to interview him. Trust me, if he is hiding something, I will know."

You can't say Roberts ain't a straight shooter. As hard as it is to hear the words, I have to appreciate him telling me like it is. I do feel better knowing his tactics were to get me to give them some kind of verbal verification to support my accusations and not necessarily that he was doubting me. The thought that Zane could be guilty but walk free terrified me. His tracks may be well covered, but there has to be a slip up somewhere. Nobody is that good.

"I'm sorry I can't be of more help. I wish I remembered something more, but I just can't." Roberts gives me a sympathetic look, "You did great, Megan, don't beat yourself up. Now I am going to bring you down to a private holding room. A doctor will be along shortly to take some tests. You stay there until I come and get you later, okay?" Slowly, my initial view of him was changing. Roberts may have been battered down by life, but a good man still resided under that tired skin. I have a new feeling towards him; I think it is admiration.

"Yeah, that's fine, thank you." As I stand up, the supervising cop looks relieved it is over and sighs as he makes his way to the door. I follow behind Roberts and we make our way back out to the noisy corridor. The universe's cruel coincidental timing is clearly at play as I take a look to my right, and there, handcuffed and being escorted by two officers, is Zane. As our eyes meet, there is a momentary pause in time. The surrounding noise quietens as everything moves in slow motion. I am rooted to the ground as he passes. The look in his eyes screams 'Help Me'. The silence is broken as his voice cuts through.

"Megan, what is going on? Will you tell them they've made a mistake?" His pleas are ones of pity. It's strange; this guy who I would have died for just yesterday now makes my blood run cold. I feel no empathy for him. I don't believe his charade for one second. I just look at him. He is close to tears and I say nothing. I just think to myself, *They have you now, motherfucker*. He continues his pleas long after he has passed and is being lead down the corridor.

"You alright? Sorry about that." Roberts places his hand on my shoulder.

"Yeah, I am fine. I'm actually glad I got to look him dead in the eye because now I have no doubt it has been him all along."

Diary Entry:

My imaginary friend died today.

I am devastated.

Baz Black

CHAPTER TWELVE

The doctor takes swabs and blood for testing. I'm positive they will find something in my system besides alcohol. As he finishes his long list of questions, he packs up his medical bag, carefully writing my name on each test tube label to be sent to the lab. Finally, he leaves and I am alone. *Jesus, Megan, this is some mess you've gotten yourself into. How were you so oblivious to not know it was him? You will be the laughing stock of the world when this gets out. I thought you were street smart? All these fancy dressing rooms and penthouse apartments have made you soft girl.* My subconscious was back to give me shit, telling it like it is.

I silence the voice with thoughts of Spike. I just can't get my head around it. If Zane went over to my apartment but knew I was still in his, then why would he have a need to kill Spike? Maybe Spike wouldn't let him in. He was really strict about that; actually he prided himself on it. If that was the case, then why did Zane want to get into my apartment so badly? My laptop is the only thing there that could possibly be what he was after. Whatever reason or scenario I can think of, nothing comes close to justifying the taking of Spike's life. When this news comes out, his family will know it's my fault that his life was taken doing the job he loved. Did Zane wait in the shadows for his shift to finish and then pounce on him like a lion killing his prey?

A new memory surfaces – as Zane was leaving that night, he had put on a black hoodie over his shirt. Was this something or nothing? Did he want the hood to conceal his face? I wanted to tell Roberts but then remember his words of conjecture. He needed evidence, not speculation. I wished once more that I had my cell phone. I'd say poor Paul is losing his mind trying to contact me. For the first time, I wonder how the guys are going to take the news about Zane. I mean, they are just like brothers, and they have known him far longer than me. Will they take his side? Maybe they will blame me? I wonder how it's going in the interview room. Has he cracked? Maybe right now he is telling them the whole sordid story. How I would love to be a fly on that wall.

One thing is for sure, I can't go back to a life of not knowing. If he lies his way out of it and they can't convict him, I will have to move away, far away. I know it's him; I saw it in his eyes. The eyes are the window to the soul and for the first time in years I saw his for what it truly was. That image of the severed goat's head that I now know was done by his hand just didn't seem as scary anymore. He is just pathetic. My career would have to take a different path, but as weak as I have felt these past few days, I know I am strong enough to start again. Maybe I will go live with 'Crazy John' and his bears. A life off grid might actually be a pleasant change of pace. I'd rather take my chances living out there amongst the wolves than the wolves that reside in this city.

A couple of hours pass and I am driving myself demented, torturing my brain with concoctions of absurdity. My torture is broken from a knock at the door. I jump back into reality. The door creaks open. It's Roberts and he is looking gaunt.

"Okay Megan, I don't think we need you to stick around any longer. We can have an officer take you home if you like." It's not the news I was expecting.

"But what happened? Is it definitely him? Did he kill Spike?" My questions spew out in one breath. I need to know. Roberts rubs his tired eyes. I can tell he has a splitting headache and I wasn't helping it.

"I'm sorry, but I can't say anything about it right now. I can tell you that we are holding him for forty-eight hours." I can only conclude that it is not going well, otherwise he would surely have some positive news for me.

"And what happens after forty-eight hours?"

"Either we charge him with something or we will have to release him." The look on his face tells me that they have nothing on him. An officer arrives with Jake; welcomingly I take him into my arms. "Get that phone of yours charged. If I have any news, I will call you." With that, he turns and heads off back down the corridor. I follow the officer and we make our way to the main exit doors. Through the glass, I can see a large crowd gathered. It looks like a protest of some sort is happening. As we step outside, I quickly realize it isn't a protest; it's a swarm of reporters and journalists. They bark my name and the familiar camera sounds begin clicking at a frantic pace.

"Megan, is it true they are holding Zane Norton as the prime suspect?"

"Did he murder Spike Howard?"

"Did you have any idea it was him stalking you?"

Questions fire from all angles. The officer pulls me off to the side as the crowd follows in unison. I remember Robert's words and don't respond to any of the incessant questions. We make it to a squad car and he ushers me in. I sit and stare out from the back window as photographers push and tussle with each other to get the best shot. This is exactly what I was dreading, but had no idea it would be so immediate. How had they even found out? This means the guys at the shop already know or they soon will. The engine starts up, and slowly we edge our way out of the parking lot avoiding masses of bodies in our way.

"That was crazy. Are you alright, Megan?"

"Yeah, I'm fine, thanks. Just wasn't expecting that." My new assigned bodyguard resembles Eddie Murphy both in looks and his fast-paced speech. I don't think now is the right time to bring it up. I'm sure he already hears enough about it from his colleagues.

"My name is Officer Jones. You need anything, just ask." We pull up outside my apartment block. I am horrified by the site of the yellow crime scene tape flapping in the wind. The true realization of Spike's meaningless death hits me hard. When word gets out that it's my fault that he was murdered, I will be hated by everyone who knew and loved him. The moment I get out of the car, cameras start clicking once again. A few paparazzi had obviously thought it was worth waiting it out here as opposed to the cop station. I ignore the lenses as I rush to the door. There I am greeted by the other doorman Jack.

"Hey Megan, how you holding up?"

"I'm okay, I'm just shocked about poor Spike."

Ink Princess

"We all are. He was a good man. Just to let you know, I had to let the cops into your apartment earlier." I hadn't even thought that they would want to check out my place for any evidence.

"Oh okay, I'm heading up there now. Thanks Jack." I already feel the weight of guilt that his friend was dead because of me.

"No problem, you take care now."

It feels so strange walking back into my apartment, like there is a heaviness in the air. I can tell there has been a disruption to my compulsive order. I let Jake down and he seems happy to be home as he rubs up against the walls as he walks. The first thing I notice is my laptop is gone; the forensics must have taken it for testing. Jones wanders behind me having a quick look around.

"Everything okay here? I will leave you to it, and I'll make sure the guys downstairs don't let anybody up." I am a little surprised.

"Oh, you aren't staying?"

"No, sorry, I have to get back to the station." I realize I sound needy, which is totally out of character for me, but then again these last few days have been an out of character experience.

"Okay, no problem. Thank you, officer." I try and recover my dignity with a carefree tone.

As soon as he closes the door, I instinctively go to fill Jake's food bowl. He comes trotting as soon as he hears me open the box.

"I'm sorry, you must be starving. Mommy hasn't been looking after you very well, has she?" I stroke his back as he devours his meal. I leave him to it and go in search of my phone charger. I shudder at the thought of Zane being here, going through my stuff. Was he here after he took Spike's life? Did he look in my mirror and realize what he had just done? I knew at this moment that my safe haven apartment was gone. There was no way I could stay here after this.

I am relieved to see the plug is still in the wall beside my bed. It's funny how our idea of power is condensed into a little white lead these days. Without this lead we feel powerless, just like I have felt. Our connection with the outside world is cut off. How did we connect before the advancement of technology? As I push the connection into my phone and see the lights start up, I do feel a rush of satisfaction. Messages fill the screen along with dozens of missed calls. Seventy-four of those missed calls are from Paul. Before I delve into the numerous mails, I decide it's only fair to call Paul first. He answers on the first ring, like he was just waiting for my call.

"Megan, Jesus Christ, I have been trying to get hold of you forever."

"I know, I'm sorry, Paul. My phone was dead and I have been at the cop station all day."

"What is going on? Nobody will tell me anything for definite, but I heard they arrested Zane?" "Yeah, it's true. It was him all along, Paul. How fucking stupid was I?" There is a pause on the line as he chooses his words carefully.

"Look, nobody saw that coming. Don't beat yourself up about it, kid. I thought Zane was such a nice guy. Just goes to show that you can't trust anyone in this world. Now, I hate to talk business at a time like this, but the media is in a frenzy and we are going to have to prepare you for a statement."

"There is no statement to give because I have no clue what is going on right now, Paul." My words come out frustrated.

"I know, and I'm sorry for bringing it up, but if we don't give these vultures something from our side, they are just going to go ahead and make it up themselves. It's already happening and I can't control it."

"Let them then; this is my life we are talking about. It's not some entertainment piece. A good man is dead because of me."

"Listen, I understand. I am just trying to look out for you. Do you want to meet up and talk?" "Are you looking out for what's best for me or you?" I cut him off as he tries to answer, "Look, I will speak to you when I am ready, but right now I just want to be left alone." I hang up and still feel the anger running through my body. It feels good to get some anger out, even if it was slightly misdirected at Paul. I meant it though – the media are at the bottom of my concerns right now.

I open up my inbox and my anger switches right back to fear as my screen is filled with Sammy's name. My hand trembles as I scroll down through dozens of texts. I randomly select ones to read through the list.

'A painter should begin every canvas with a wash of black, because all things in nature are dark except where exposed by the light.'
'Art washes away from the soul the dust of everyday life.'
'Art is not what you see, but what you make others see.'

Every message I open has a subliminal art quote. As I scroll to the top, again my heart starts beating hard as I notice the timeline. The last text was sent ten minutes ago, the one before it twenty minutes ago. I trace back ten texts and all are sent ten minutes apart. It can't be Zane; he's been in custody for over three hours now. I scroll down further to confirm the pattern of texts go back hours. I feel numb.

As fast as my finger allows, I dial Roberts' cell. As I lift the phone up to my ear, I swiftly drop it as I hear a noise from the kitchen. My rational reasoning knows it's just Jake, but my irrational reasoning feels someone is in the apartment. I cautiously make my way to the bedroom door. I listen but no further noise comes. *C'mon Jake, show yourself to be the creator of the gentle bang I just heard.* My whole body rattles with shock as my phone vibrates against the glass top of my bedside table. It must be Roberts calling me back. I turn to retrieve it, but my footsteps are halted as a hand grabs me violently by the mouth. I try to turn around, but some form of cloth covers my mouth. It is wet and pungent, clasped tight. I arch my back as I struggle against the force, but my efforts are short lived. My eyes roll back into my head and the fight in my body relaxes. I feel blackness wash over me as my limp body falls back into their arms.

Diary Entry:

I don't necessarily want to die. I just want the pain to go away. To close my eyes and to not have to feel anything anymore is a notion I flirt with every day. What is my purpose? To sit on this man made concrete and rot away? Maybe I am just not meant for this world. It seems the universe has rejected me. If it wasn't for my painting, I would have nothing, a cruel gift bestowed upon me. A creative mind is always searching, searching for inspiration, searching for answers. I wonder what it would feel like to be normal. Maybe I am normal and have delusions of grandeur?

Selling my art is like selling my soul. My paintings are a part of me and I find it foreign that a complete stranger would want to own a part of me. None of the great artists ever did it for the money (I am not in the category of great artists). They did it because it's all they knew. All

I know at this moment is selling my pieces is the only way I can survive out here. My body is covered in sores, this winter has taken its toll on my frail body. I define the definition of skin and bones. My cheeks have sunken in so badly that my bones threaten to protrude from my skin. I'm really not sure how much longer I can last out here. My will is starting to crack and I don't know how to repair it. If anybody finds this diary with my body, I wonder if they will even bother to read it? Ramblings of a street rat is probably not worthy of anybody's time. I never read back on what I have written in here. I think it would scare me too much. I just have to get these thoughts out of my head somehow. I don't really have anybody to talk to out here. It's like being stranded out at sea, surrounded by water but unable to drink any of it. I know if I go down the route of talking to myself out loud, I will have admitted defeat to my mental stability. I will try and sleep now. If the universe hears my pleas, then maybe it will take me as a sacrifice. I am ready and willing...

CHAPTER THIRTEEN

The blackness is fading from my eyes and flickers of light break through. A sharp pain nestles at the back of my head. The overpowering stench of liquid still lingering on my lips stings my nostrils. Through the stench, another familiar smell forces its way through. It's the smell of mold, the same smell that was on the artwork left for me, the same smell that lingered in the hallway after my stalker's visits. My eyes open to no more than a strained squint. My surroundings are dank and squalid. A solitary low hanging lamp is the only source of light. I try to move my hand to rub my stinging eyes but am now aware my hands are both restrained behind my back. I shake my head to try get the fuzziness clear from my brain.

As my eyes and senses begin to even out, I can now see countless easels displaying artwork scattered across the vast loft space. A faint sound of opera music comes from far away. The mold smell really hits me now; I can taste it in my mouth. I am bound to a wooden chair by thick rope wrapped tightly around my ankles. My panic caused by claustrophobia sets in and I squirm to break free. The more I move, the tighter the rope gets. I know he has finally gotten me, after seven years. Strangely, I feel a sense of relief that the not knowing part was over. Even if this was my final hour, I feel a sense of freedom from the constant worry and stress over what lurked in the shadows. The absurdity of my situation does not escape me. My life has turned into the stuff of movies (or nightmares) these past few days, and this is its dramatic climax.

I study the crude artwork around the room; similar paintings to what this creep had left for me adorn the canvases. Sacrificed animals and blood are the main theme that runs through each. It is not the time to critique, but they really all looked so forced, done by somebody with no natural talent.

I hear hurried footsteps coming up the stairs. In a glint of hope, I imagine the entire New York Police Department descending on the building to come to my rescue. Instead, all I see is a balding head emerging from the stairwell. A short, plump figure walks towards me. I can't make out any detail of his face in the dim lighting. My head throbs with unbearable pain.

"Oh, you are awake. Sorry, you must be so scared." The voice matches the phone call from the show (dispelling Roberts' theory of a device being used). How will Zane ever forgive me? Even in my death, he will never forget what I did to him. I mistook coincidence for circumstance.

"I wanted everything to be just perfect for you." I stay silent and squint to make out his face as he slowly approaches.

"Don't worry, I'm not going to hurt you. I am here to save you." A part of me searching for hope wants to believe him, but I know it's a lie. He is now standing in front of me with his arm stretched out to assure me that he means no harm. Now I can see his face. This unassuming face is the face that has tormented me for all these years.

Every time I tried to imagine what he looked like, this was not what was in my mind. As I study him closely, I feel I have met him before, but can't quite place it.

"I'm sorry I had to do this to you, but I was worried you wouldn't understand."

"There are people looking for me, you know." It's my first words to my perpetrator, and surprisingly I don't feel any fear towards him. Actually, he looks more scared than me. He rubs his head hard.

"I knew it, I knew they would have brainwashed you. They are trying to hurt you, Megan. I am here to protect you. I will make you see that."

"Who exactly is trying to hurt me?"

"Them, they are; I see them plotting and planning." I can now see he is deranged and decide I have to play this one smart if I am to get out of here alive. This psychopath murdered Spike, but I have to contain my anger and feed his delusions with cooperation.

"Okay, well thank you for saving me then." His frustrated expression changes to relief.

"You believe me now? I have protected you from the very first time we met. I could see the danger you were in and I knew what I had to do." My inkling of having met this creep before was right. I know better than to ask where, as he will surely be offended if I can't remember him. I try to word it so that he tells me.

"I knew we had a connection that time. I had no idea you were the one protecting me for all these years." He looks confused and scratches his head with his filthy overgrown nails.

"But you wouldn't even look at me that day. I saw the real you on the canvas. Nobody else saw it. I knew you needed my help."

Before I can come up with an answer to continue my charade, he darts off to the side of the room. His sudden burst of movement makes me nervous for the first time. Is he on to me? Has he gone to retrieve an instrument that will now end my life? I wait in anticipation. He returns moments later carrying a white sheet. The sight of this makes me shift upright in the hard seat. I watch anxiously as he reaches under the sheet. I prepare my body for impending pain, but to my relief he pulls out three canvases, instead of a blunt lump hammer.

To my utter disbelief, the paintings on the canvases are mine. The memory that was locked away comes pouring out. I am looking at the 'art critic' from my exhibition in Art Nouveau, all those years ago. He is still wearing his disgusting tweed jacket he had on that day. Balder now than back then, but still the same creepy face, boiled and blistered. He was right – I had avoided eye contact with him that day because he kept staring at me with his beady little eyes. Was he even a critic or just some randomer that happened to be in the gallery that day? He was obviously the mystery winning bidder from the auction. I hate that I had spent this creep's money.

"You see, I have kept you here all these years, safe with me. I had to buy them at any cost. I knew how badly you needed that money." I didn't need your fucking charity, I'd rather starve and die than take money off you. He continues his deluded ramblings and I hold my tongue.

"How those other idiots didn't realize that this was you in the painting baffles me. I knew right away. Those stuck up assholes can't see past the nose on their face. How could they not see your pain, your cry for help?"

He makes me feel sick as he speaks. I refrain from pointing out that Lou also knew it was me. I can sense how unstable this lunatic is.

"Did you like the art that I did for you?" He looks at me with a hopefulness in his eyes, but I imagine his expression could change very quickly if I gave him the wrong answer.

"Oh, yes, it was very creative." I hope my lame attempt at a lie pacifies him.

"I know I have nowhere near your talent, but maybe in time you can teach me." *In time* – he actually thinks he is going to keep me here as his prisoner. I think I would rather him kill me than that prospect.

"Can I ask why you never approached me face to face over all the years?" *Dangerous, Megan, be careful how far you push this guy.*

"Oh, I couldn't. They were always watching you. That's why I had to sneak into your apartment today to get you out of there undetected. Again, I am so sorry I had to do it that way, but it was the only option I had. Luckily, I know every inch of that building. I have studied it long and hard and their security systems are pathetic." I so badly want to lay it out straight to this maniac, tell him how he has destroyed my life, but I hold it all in.

"And the phone call when I was on the TV show the other night, why then?" He scratches his head, this time so hard he draws blood from his forehead.

"I needed them to know I was your protector. They were planning their move and I needed to prevent it." I wince as his disgusting blood runs down his blotched skin; the sight makes me feel queasy.

I have to ask, "Who are 'they' and why are they trying to get me?"

"It's complicated, hard to explain. I know things, things I would be killed for knowing. If it wasn't for me, they would have gotten to you long ago. I just wanted you to know I wouldn't let them harm you. You know they took my daughter? I wasn't there to save her, but I'm here for you, and have been for all these years." As he speaks it's clear that he truly believes he is protecting me, but really he has fabricated a story to justify his stalking.

"I'm sorry to hear about your daughter. How old was she when they took her?" Now he looks at me as if I am a stranger.

"How did you know they took my daughter?"

"You just told me about her a minute ago." He scratches his face with both hands, his long nails digging in hard.

"I was afraid of this. Where is it?"

"Where is what?" I was growing concerned over his agitated state.

"The implant, where did they put it?"

"I have no idea what you are talking about. Now why don't you show me some of your paintings?" My effort to distract him fails.

"No, don't make me look for it, please. Just tell me where it is and I won't have to hurt you."

"There is no implant, I swear to you." He storms off to the back of the room, leaving me terrified. *Stupid girl, why did you push him?* As he returns, I notice a small black leather pouch tucked under his arm.

"Last chance, Megan. I don't want to hurt you, just tell me where it is."

"Look at me, look into my eyes. I am telling you there is no implant. They never got to me. Please, you have to believe me." I begin to sob as he shakes his head and rolls open his leather case displaying an array of rusted medical instruments.

"I'm sorry, I have to find it." He pours a bottle of liquid onto a handkerchief and places it over my mouth. My screams are muffled until again my eyes roll back and I pass out.

A burning pain shoots through my body. "I'm sorry, I'm so sorry, I should never have doubted you; please forgive me." His words are blurred through my disorientated state. I force my heavy head up and try to shake off the drool from my mouth. The more I come around, the worse the pain gets, a burning pain that I can't quite locate to one particular area. Through blurred vision I can see blood. Crimson blood covers my hands, which are now untied. I make several attempts to speak before any words come out.

"What, what did you do to me?" I can hear him pacing back and forth.

"I had to check, I had to make sure they didn't get to you. They are so crafty. It's okay, you are all clear."

My vision adjusts; I am soaking wet with blood. My arms have been hacked to pieces with incisions in his search for the imaginary implant. I feel warm blood trickling down my back from my neck and the open wounds sting in the stale air. I hear him running water as he mutters to himself. He returns with a basin and wash cloths.

"I'm just going to clean you up. Don't worry, it looks worse than it is. I was very careful." He begins gently washing the blood from my arms, my tattoos invisible under the thick dry plasma. The warm water burns as it soaks into the gaping wounds. I squirm in my chair and he rubs his hand on my head.

"Hush now, it's okay. I will get you cleaned up." His disgusting hand rubbing my head feels worse than the pain.

"I need to get to a hospital." He stops cleaning and throws the blood soaked cloth down.

"Now Megan, you know we can't go there. The doctors are all in on it. Who do you think pays their wages? No, I will look after you here where it's safe" My heart sinks; I know I will die here.

"Please, I need some water." My mouth is dry and my body dehydrated.

"Of course, sorry, I should have gotten you some already. Hold on, I'll be right back."

I wait for him to disappear back down the stairs and muster up any energy left in my body to reach down and pull at the rope binding my feet. Blood drips to the floor as my head leans down. I frantically struggle with the knot, but it's too tight. I am concentrating so hard on the rope I forget my balance and the weight of my head tips forward; my full body weight crashes to the floor still attached to the chair. My hands break the fall a little, but my head still thuds into the wooden floorboards. I begin to sob. This could have been my only chance of escape and I just failed. I hear him running back up the stairs to investigate the commotion.

"Megan, are you okay? What happened?" He awkwardly picks me up and leans me back into the chair.

"I think I passed out," hoping he will buy the excuse through my tears.

"Here, drink this." He places the grubby glass to my mouth and pours the metallic room temperature water in. I struggle to hold the liquid and half of it spills out of my mouth before I can swallow.

"Can you untie my feet, please? I'm not going anywhere." He studies me for a moment and then looks sympathetic.

"Of course, I'm sorry, it was just for your own safety." With that he begins untying my legs. As he pulls the rope away, I stretch them out to try to get some blood flowing again.

"Thank you." Got to keep him on my side; it's my only hope. He picks up the bloody cloth and starts cleaning my neck with it. The water has gone cold and makes me shiver all over.

"So, is this where you live?" Have to keep him talking.

"Oh no, this is just my work space. We will go to my house later. I think you are going to love it. And best of all, they can't find you there. I've seen to that."

I already know the answer, but I try and test him anyway, "There will be people worried about me. When it's safe can I let them know I'm okay?"

He guffaws, "What, like Zane? He's working for them, Megan. I saw him last night, planting chips in your apartment. I almost had him too, but..."

I couldn't help myself, I needed to know. "But what?"

"Just as I was about to grab him, that fucking doorman spotted me. Don't let his age fool you; he's been working for them a long time. I dealt with him." I try so hard not to react to his admission to killing Spike, but I let out one short gasped cry. He looks surprised at my reaction. I nod my head to keep him talking.

"I see the cops have Zane now. They have no clue who he really is. They will release him and he will come looking for you. Don't worry, though. He's never going to get to you again."

As horrible as the situation is, I am glad to finally be getting some answers to the mayhem. I know I shouldn't push him, but there is one answer I really needed to know and this may be my only chance to ask it.

"Can I ask you about the emails from Sammy's phone?" He smiles at me; the first smile I have seen from him. His teeth are stained yellow and crooked.

"Oh yes, that was genius, wasn't it? There was no way they would suspect one of their own. That way I could contact you without fear of getting caught."

Again, I play along with his delusions to get the answer I was looking for, "You mean, Sammy was one of them?"

A look of pride washes over his face, "Oh yes, that's why he had to die." This time I can't hold my emotions and tears stream down my face.

"What's wrong? I was protecting you. He was going to do really bad things. I tapped his phone; I heard the conversations. That's when I knew I had to cut his brakes and stop him. I know it's hard for you because you think these people are your friends, but they are trying to hurt you, and I'm the only one who can stop them." I try to control my tears, but they keep flowing.

"So you took his phone after the crash?"

"Yes, I followed him to make sure it all went according to plan. I took his phone to analyze. It was full of cryptic codes that I have spent years working on to decipher, but they are a highly intelligent and sophisticated operation." I try to not look sullen as it might trigger another outburst, but my anguish just won't stay in. His unstable mind always a trigger-pull away from exploding. Not for the first time today, I consider my chances of making a run for it. His robust frame would not be fast, but my body felt weak from blood loss. I could make it halfway and collapse, and then surely he would put an end to my life, his paranoia convincing him that I was working for 'them'.

My eyes scan the vast room looking for exits and weapons. Then my mind focuses on the glass that he had left in my hands. Could I muster up enough energy to deliver a fatal blow upon his bald head? I would finish the job with shards of glass, making sure to puncture an artery. I would watch him squirm and gasp for breath like a fish on dry land, payback for taking my friends' lives. I let him babble on while I make silent, deadly plans.

"I have lovely fresh clothes for you back at the house. You can even take a bath if you wish."

"That would be nice." I'd wait for his arched back to be turned and slam this glass down hard, as hard as my might would allow. Sure, I might injure my hand in the process, but it was a minor sacrifice for not only my freedom but my vengeance.

"First, I have to stitch these up for you or they may end up infected." I grimace as he produces a crude sewing kit. His putrid breath makes me turn my head away as he begins threading the needle through the flaps of skin on my arms.

"Now, I may have to check the rest of your body later on for implants. Normally it's always the neck or arms, but they will go to any lengths to trick me, always advancing. Don't worry, we can do it together this time." He puffs and sweats as he attends to the numerous incisions. The needle pricks and prods as it passes through, but it does feel better to have the gaping wounds closed tight. His filthy hands are now covered in my blood. I worry he has passed his bacteria into my body, but there is nothing I can do about it right now. When I finally look down to examine his work, I see my skin has been pulled together in a crude manner, uneven and coarse. If left like this, I will surely scar, scars that will remind me of this day forever. He picks up the blood soaked cloth and wipes off the last of the blood from my arms.

"I'm so glad you are finally here. For years I have dreamed of this day. I wanted it to be perfect. I know it will take some time to adjust to, but anything you wish or desire I will make sure you have it." He holds my left cheek in his hand, rubbing his thumb up and down. I fight the urge to pull away but can't bring myself to make eye contact.

"Why won't you look at me, Megan? After everything I have done for you, I think you owe me at least that." His words sound hurt and verging on anger. I know I need to say the right thing to make sure I still have my opportunity to pounce.

"I know, I'm sorry. I am grateful; I am just scared, that's all." I force my eyes to meet his. They are clouded, like someone who has stayed in darkness for too long. I suppose that's where he liked to be, hidden, lurking in the shadows.

"But why? You are safe now; for the first time in years you are safe. I promise you they won't harm you." Forced, everything is forced. I contract my jaw muscles to raise a smile and then make my first move.

"Can we go to your house now? I really would like that bath."

His turn to smile, but his is real, "Sure, we can do that. You will love it there."

I knew I had to make my escape here. If he got me to his house, who knows what sort of prison cell awaited me. I tighten my grip around the glass and without looking down try to work out the best angle to deliver the blow. My sweaty hands loosen my grip. One by one, I wipe them on my jeans to try to soak up the moisture. Every muscle tenses up in my tired body, the adrenaline counteracts the pain at least. Like a cobra preparing to strike, I erect my body as much as possible from my seated position. Just as I feel I am ready for my attack, my plans are thwarted in an instant as I see him pour more of the terrible liquid onto a rag. *Think fast, Megan.*

"Eh, what are you doing?"

He darts his eyes toward me as I interrupt his task, "It's the only way, I'm afraid. I just can't risk them seeing you. It will be the last time I have to do it, I promise. Once you are safe with me, there will be no need for you to ever leave." He slowly approaches me with the rag held down low at his waist to avoid inhaling the toxic fumes himself.

"But I'll be careful. You can just tell me exactly what to do and I will do it. Please, there is no need for this." My last desperate plea before I knew I would have to strike from my seated position, a distinct disadvantage.

"I'm sorry, but I just can't take that risk. We have come too far; now please don't make this hard on yourself."

Oh don't you worry, you sick, twisted fuck. I won't make it hard on myself, but you will soon be picking glass out of your eyeballs. You will be rolling around, slipping in your own blood as I repeatedly plunge glass into your pathetic body. My inner monologue psyching myself up to deliver the task at hand. Moments now. The glass rattles in my hands, a last minute decision to take it in my right hand and down to my side. More momentum with just the one hand. A blow to the temple is now my target. This is it, close enough now. I raise my trembling hand, but just as I am about to swing it, a deafening 'BANG' echoes through the loft. The structure shakes and my grip on the glass releases. I watch as it shatters against the hard floor. My ears are deafened from the noise and the glass makes no sound.

He steps away from me now, panicked. I see tiny lights dancing on the wall at the far end of the loft. Then something appears from the staircase entrance. I can see movement but can't make out what it is. Then, more lights; following the lights are black helmets, machine guns drawn. Dozens now fill the open floor space. I didn't notice him slide around behind me, too distracted by the tiny lights coming to save me. A simple raise of an arm from the leader stops the SWAT team from descending towards us. I implore them to keep moving with my eyes. I daren't call out as now he has something cold and sharp pressed against the bulging artery on the side of my neck. Guns are still drawn and pointing in my direction. Please just shoot him. Get me out of here! *Don't move, Megan.*

"Stay back, you aren't taking her." I struggle to hear his words over the ringing in my head. And then through the army of black clad bodies emerges the welcome sight of Detective Roberts. For the first time I have seen, he wears an expression of concern.

"Megan, are you alright?" I can't move my mouth to answer as the sharpness of the instrument pushes hard against my skin. It wouldn't take much to tear it open.

"Of course she is alright. Do you really think I would hurt her? I am her protector against you. I won't let you take her. I promised I would take care of her."

Roberts switches to playing along with the charade. "Of course you wouldn't hurt her; that's why you need to take the scalpel away from her neck, George." This is the first time I hear his name. Roberts knows who he is. Even if I die right now, I am somewhat relieved that someone will be able to tell the real story of what happened me.

"You are just trying to trick me, like you people always do. But I'm smart, not like the others. I know she would rather die by my hand than let you take her away for your experiments."

Roberts takes a step closer every time he speaks, "Listen, George, we are not with them. In fact, we are deep undercover and we need your help. You are the only one with the skillset to infiltrate them. We don't have much time. You can walk out of here with Megan, that's no problem. We are just here to ask for your help." Roberts instructs the army behind him to lower their guns with a wave of his hand. I can see from the corner of my eye he is scratching his head in angst just like earlier.

"Why should I believe you? This is what they do, mind control." The pressure of the blade lessens as he battles his confusion.

"I know it is; they did the same to me, but I got away and now I head up a secret organization to bring these bastards down. Look, George, I know you don't want to hurt Megan. We can all walk out of here and we will let you take her to safety. All that I ask is you join us. I don't think we can win without your help." The scalpel moves off of my neck now. Roberts keeps his stare on George and lifts his finger to me directing me not to move. I wait with bated breath.

Shouting now, "They said you would do this! I won't let you take her from me!" I crouch downwards as his roar frightens me, and then a single soft gunshot rings out through the air. I hear a thud and look around to see George lying on his back, no movement. Roberts rushes towards me and pulls me from my seat. My legs wobble as he barges his way through the oncoming rush of the SWAT team. He doesn't stop until we reach the back of the room.

"You are okay, Megan. I've got you." I collapse into his chest sobbing hard. He repeats his words, "I've got you."

CHAPTER FOURTEEN

Three months have now passed since the incident. A lot has changed in that time; most of all, I have changed. Of course the events of that day were going to affect me, but through adversity I found some form of solace. Roberts insisted I see a specialist psychiatrist, and he set it up for me. Reluctantly, I agreed, but it turned out to be life changing for me. I have spoken with psychiatrists before, but Doctor Thornton was different. He made me realize that I wasn't as immune to my past as I made myself believe. In our sessions I laid it all out on the table, something I had never done, but he made it easy, never judged or patronized me like others have done in the past. I spent so many years being numb, it felt strange to have all of these feelings and emotions return.

I actually feel more human now. I knew that I had to move, but I didn't want to feel like I was running away. Once you start running you might never stop. I stayed in New York for about a month after, but that city would never feel the same for me. I never went back to my apartment after that day. I had movers pack it all up, including Jake, and got it delivered to the hotel storage where I was to stay for the forthcoming weeks. I just could not face going back there. Even now when I think about it, those horrible feelings come creeping back to haunt me. My old apartment wasn't the only thing I couldn't face. The shop was off limits. I guess I felt shame, at least that's what I told Doctor

Thornton. I knew I had let my family down and couldn't face Zane to try and explain my actions.

I locked myself away in my hotel room. I had no cell phone or laptop, cut off from the outside world, except for the obsolete hotel telephone. I only ventured out for my visits with Doctor Thornton, and when I did, I covered my face as best I could, using strategic hat and scarf placements. I also visited Spike and Sammy's graves where I begged them for forgiveness and sobbed for hours.

It was certainly a strange couple of weeks for me, back in my own company, and not at the beck and call of the industry. I really didn't know if I was ever even going to tattoo again. Unlike before, I didn't miss it, and that scared me. I did miss my friends, my family, but I was lost. I needed to find my own way first. The media had all but given up after numerous attempts to nab me for an interview. They camped outside the hotel for days on end. Several attempts were made to get past the front desk, but the security were alert at all times. I paid them all a little extra not to be disturbed, and also for them to turn a blind eye to Jake being present in my room. I did worry that I was becoming agoraphobic. I felt safe inside my spacious room and saw no reason to leave. The outside world terrified me.

Paul had left persistent messages at reception for me to contact him. I did feel bad about not getting in touch, but I just couldn't deal with the expectation. After days of the polite receptionist informing me of all the messages that had been left for me, I requested not to be told about them anymore. Left in limbo, I knew it was killing him, but I had to put me first. That's a new credo I had learned in therapy, taking time out to concentrate on me. I know it may sound self-centered, but it's what I needed to get my head right during those weeks.

I didn't even turn on the television for fear of seeing my story on the news. I had caught glimpses of my face as I passed newspaper stalls on my brisk walk to therapy. Yes, I was curious, but never enough to buy any. I filled my day with painting and writing poetry. Jesus, how egocentric does that sound? It was therapeutic, but no matter how hard I tried, remnants of 'him' plagued my work. In my belongings down in storage I had rooted out my old Discman. I listened to CDs as I worked. (The Discman is not quite old enough to be antique and has yet to become retro.). Without my digital contraptions, reverting to this old school method of music play felt perfect.

I did find myself constantly watching the door as I worked; I daren't turn my back. I created some truly fucked up pieces during that time. I'm glad Doctor Thornton did not request to see them, as he may very well have had me committed on the spot. Diary entries and poems filled up notebook after notebook. Thoughts and feeling spilling onto the pages at a furious pace.

After almost four weeks of this, my room began to feel like my coffin. Claustrophobia slowly began to return, clawing at my skin. Similar to a prison, three square meals delivered to my door each day. I refused the interruption of housekeeping except for fresh towels delivered with my breakfast every morning.

One evening, as my breath grew shallow with panic, I escaped to the hallway. Standing there glancing up and down the long corridors, I really didn't know where to go. I still had visions of 'him' appearing, scalpel in hand. I tried to rid the fear from my body, but it resurfaced again and again. Before I knew it, I was walking towards the elevator. The feeling of empowerment making it that far was triumphant. I ventured all the way to the lobby that night, much to the surprise of the staff who had only really seen me to deliver various requests to my room. I found myself subconsciously wandering into the internet room.

Sitting down in front of the computer screen, I debated whether to click on the mouse that had found its way into my hand. I knew there was stuff on there that I was not yet ready to deal with, maybe never ready to deal with. I reasoned that my private email account should really only have my close friends' messages on there. That hadn't stopped 'him' from penetrating it, but he couldn't get to me anymore. Hesitantly, I logged in and waited for the screen to fill with unread mails. All the usual suspects were there as I scrolled through them – Lou, Frankie, Mike, Paul, just seeing their names made me miss them. One name that wasn't there was Zane. I wasn't surprised, but I was hurt. I had no right to feel that way after what I had put him through, but his lack of mail confirmed his anger towards me. Amongst the emails was a friend of mine by the name of Jeff Prime. Jeff owned Grit n Glory Tattoo out in Florida. We had met on the tattoo convention circuit and had become good friends over the years. I clicked open his email first, as it stood out.

'Hey Megan, Really sorry to hear about all the shit that went down. Listen, I am a man down here at the shop and need it filled fast. The chair is yours if you want it. I'm not sure what your plans are or anything, but if you want a change of scenery and the guys are cool with it, give me a shout, Take care, Jeff.'

This got me thinking; a change of scenery sounded good, a fresh start. I felt a wave of excitement for the first time in weeks. The prospect of such an impulsive move exhilarated me and I realized in that moment how much I missed my tattooing. I remember opening up the rest of the emails but was too distracted to register the information as my mind was already planning my move. The very next day I called Jeff from my room and put the plans in place to move my life to Florida.

I caught the Amtrak with Jake smuggled into my bag, and without incident I was on my way to a new life. I remember the heaviness falling off my shoulders as we left miles behind us. It was by no means the miracle cure, but it was definitely a step in the right direction. I kept my 'disguise' on the whole way to maintain anonymity, going to a place I hoped would no longer require one.

So here I sit in Tampa Bay, the evening sun pumping light into my pristine white apartment. I am almost afraid to say it, but I am happy. There were times back in New York that I thought I was happy, but I know now it was always closer to contentment than true happiness. My mind is clear and relaxed out here, the car noise now replaced with gulls singing for their supper. I am adjusting to life not looking over my shoulder for strangers lurking in the darkness.

The shop is great and I'm steadily building up my client base again. I get along with all my coworkers, but they are not my family. I have contacted all the guys since I've been out here, all except Zane. This was about to change in one hour as I have arranged for Zane to come here to see me. I was skeptical if I would even get a reply to my email, let alone an acceptance of my invitation. I sit here on my balcony and ponder just how I am going to explain myself. Except for Doctor Thornton, I had not discussed the events of that day with anyone, but I knew I would have to tonight; he deserved an explanation. The papers, magazines and internet all spun their own version of the story, but none of it came from me directly. I have been offered millions for the exclusive, but money is no substitute for my sanity.

Another positive thing has happened while out here, myself and Billy have decided to give it another shot. After the dust had settled, I began to realize how hard I had been on him. I actually couldn't figure out why he had stayed with me for so long. He was right, he had been dealing with a closed book, all of my emotions encapsulated inside; no matter how hard he tried, he could not get it open. I reached out to him and he reached right back. We are taking things slow. We don't dwell on the past but now look to the future. He is now seeing me in a different light as the book is finally open and I want him to read every chapter.

I made a promise to myself to tie up loose ends that I had left in New York. I wanted to prove that I moved away and didn't run away. Paul was a loose end. I had left him in perpetual limbo. He had not expected to hear my voice as he answered the unregistered number that day. He sounded genuinely concerned about my wellbeing. Understandably, he was frustrated that I hadn't contacted him. As I explained to him that I just needed some space and distance from the public eye, he sounded like he had already come to terms with it in the weeks of my absence. After I had promised to contact him as soon as I was ready, I hung up feeling relieved that he didn't scream down the phone at me. I do feel bad for not contacting him sooner; he has been really good to me through the years. Another part of the mess cleaned up.

A surprise step in dealing with my past came in the form of a letter from my estranged brother. He had posted it from prison to the shop address in New York, and the guys sent it on to me down here. I had not spoken to Jordan in over seventeen years, so it came as a total surprise to hear from him. I read the handwritten letter over and over. It was short and scribbled and some of it was hard to make out. What I could decipher was that he would be getting out soon and he wanted to come see me. He had seen the interview and said he was proud of me. It's strange how a dormant love can become active in a matter of seconds. I was really excited to see him again and wrote him a letter straight back. His parole hearing is next month, so hopefully our reunion will happen then. I have no idea what I am going to say to him, but I will cross that bridge when it comes to it.

Time was edging closer until the meeting that I didn't think would ever happen. I had arranged to meet him down at the harbor. A coffee shop seemed too formal and eye to eye contact from across a table terrified me. I was now pacing my apartment as I ran through countless monologues in my head, trying to pick one that sounded right. I kiss Jake goodbye and ask him to wish me luck.

Twenty minutes early for our seven o'clock meeting. I sit on the edge of the pier and let my legs hang over the side. Fishing boats dock after a long day out at sea. Smells vary at different times of the day down here. Tonight a gentle breeze carries in the freshness of the sea air and mixes with the ever present aroma of fish. I clutch my phone in case Zane is in need of directions. The sun has begun its descent from the sky; the orange glow tints the water below.

Distracted, I don't notice Zane until he is halfway up the pier. I do a double take as his presence takes me by surprise. I jump to my feet and awkwardly wave as his tall, skinny frame strides towards me. As he reaches me, I am not sure what to do. He extends his arms, wrapping them around me and pulls me into a deep hug. I was not expecting this, but gladly welcome it. In that moment I truly felt how much I had missed my best friend. As the embrace ends, he speaks first.

"How you been?" It feels strange. Not like before, but then how could it?

"I'm fine, thanks. Things are going pretty good out here, and how about you?" Please don't say, 'What, apart from you ruining my life that time? Yeah, it's okay.' It's too early in the conversation to get to that part.

"Oh, you know, the same old with me, not too bad I guess." Pretty vague, but better than him screaming at me I suppose.

We begin to stroll along the pier. All of my rehearsed speeches drop out of mind and I struggle to find words. After a time, walking in silence, side by side, I offer a gentle, "I'm so sorry." These are not the words I was looking for. Sorry seems flippant against the gravity of the situation that I had put him in.

"Listen, it's okay. I have had a lot of time to think about and I realize the pressure you were under. But just for you to think it was me, it does fucking hurt. I'm not going to lie and pretend it doesn't." We stop at the end of the pier and both sit down on the wooden bench without a word or a gesture towards it.

"It's not okay. What I did will never be okay. You are my best friend in the world and I've ruined it. I have gone over it and over it. I have so much to say to you, but can never find the right words. My only defense is that I was out of my mind that day. I think the pressure and the stress had finally taken over. It's still no excuse, but I started connecting pieces that didn't really exist. Deep down I didn't want to believe it was you, but on the surface my emotions tricked me into believing it." He looks down and fiddles with his hands. I wait for him to speak.

"Did you really think I was capable of murder? After so many years of knowing me better than anyone does, did you think I was capable of taking a life?" I can tell this has been the question burning inside him for months. He deserves an honest answer.

"Yes, at the time I did. I hated thinking it, believing you were capable of it, but I had convinced myself you were not the person I thought I knew." He laughs out with a disbelief exhale, shaking his head.

"I'm sorry, Zane, but you deserve the truth. I will understand if you never want to speak to me again. I'm still shocked that you even agreed to meet me. I am prepared to tell you everything. I have kept quiet about it all these months as no one really deserves to know the details, but you do."

"Listen, Megan, even after everything that happened, I still care deeply about you and I missed my crazy friend being around. You don't have to explain yourself if you don't want to. After the cops released me, that Detective Roberts briefly told me what had happened." One thing was for sure, I could never be as understanding as he is being right now.

"I want to explain; I want to let you know what was happening inside my head. I want you to try and understand."

He turns to face me for the first time, "Okay then, if you are sure." Where do I start? These words had been locked inside my head for weeks. Now I needed to find a cohesive way of letting them out.

"Okay, so just bear with me here. I'm really not sure how this is going to sound to you. I will try my best to explain what was going through my head. Obviously, I was freaked out the night we went for dinner. I hadn't eaten properly in days and the cocktails went straight to my head. We got back to your place and then you remembered Jake. You put me to bed and headed off to go and get him. I woke in the middle of the night and I still felt horrible from the alcohol. The lights weren't working and I was scared. I was worried that something had happened to you and went down to check if you were back. When I saw you typing on the laptop in the dark, you slammed it down as soon as you saw me. I asked you what you were doing and you said, 'Catching up on some work stuff.' Then when I went looking for my phone in my bag, you claimed you hadn't seen it, but it was clearly on the table beside your laptop. Then I got you to read the text out on my phone from Sammy. Your reaction kind of shocked me when you said, 'At least he is trying to protect you and not hurt you.' It felt like you were sticking up for this creep. But still, up until that point I wasn't thinking anything malicious about you." Zane is maintaining eye contact with me and listening, but I can see his lips tremor as he is dying to fight his case. He lets me continue.

"I went to sleep feeling crappy and then you woke me with breakfast in bed and you were being lovely to me. After my shower I came down to the kitchen and offered to help you clean up. You said it was fine and to just relax. You still had my cell and had left it on the table. When I went to check it the battery was dead. I mentioned going to my apartment to get the charger and that's when things went downhill. You starting telling me it was best to stay inside and to not turn my phone on even though you knew I needed to speak with Roberts. When I starting walking towards the elevator, you grabbed me by the shoulders and led me back to the couch. Right then, I saw—well at least I thought I saw—something in you that had been hidden from me."

I continued, "I was already in the depths of paranoia and my deluded mind starting linking you. I know how fucked up it sounds, but I couldn't help it. I thought about how protective you were over me and how you never seemed to like my boyfriends. How the timelines all pieced together. We knew this creep was good with computers, which you are. You paint as a hobby, so that explained the art he left for me. Then I started linking absurdities to reality, like when I came back from the bathroom at the restaurant and you had your hand over my drink. Well, I'm sorry, but I told Roberts that I thought you may have drugged me." At this point Zane shakes his head and grits his teeth. I don't wait for a further reaction and just continue. If I don't get this all out now, I may never will.

"I know it's a horrible thing to say, but I just felt so out of it that night; passing out in the cab just added to my suspicions. So I began concocting the whole story in my head, that it was you who had tormented me all those years and I was too blind and stupid to see it. I didn't have a real reason to back up my theory, but I suppose I considered that you may have had feelings for me that I didn't reciprocate. I concluded that what you were doing on your laptop that night was texting my phone from Sammy's number. I was sitting there in your apartment pretending to paint and I actually believed I was your prisoner. I'm ashamed to admit that when you went to get the art supplies I was planning my escape even if it meant hurting you. The moment you left the room, I had sprung up to try the elevator, but it was locked. Again, this excelled my delusion that I was trapped. I had strongly considered hurting you to make my escape."

I take a quick breath and continue, "Then when Roberts came looking for me, I was so relieved. I thought he was saving me from you. Even when you hugged me and said, 'I will be here waiting for you,' I took it as a threat, and not words of support from my friend. As soon as I got into the car with Roberts, I starting regurgitating my fantastical story. He fed into my confirmation when he told me Spike had been murdered. I then told him how you had gone over there and I had no clue what time you got back. I thought he might have stopped you getting into my apartment and you killed him. I'm so sorry, Zane. At the time it all made perfect sense. I can see now how absurd it all sounds. I was so scared and confused, but it's still no excuse for what I did to you. I will never forget that look on your face as the cops brought you down that hallway. I don't expect you to ever forgive me, but I just wanted to try and explain." My mouth has run dry; the difficult words have come out in some form.

Zane pauses, "Wow, that is a lot to take in. I mean, the cops only told me half of that stuff. They just kept repeating the same questions over and over, trying to make me slip up. They never told me that it was you directly that thought it was me. Now it makes sense why they were asking me about what medicine I had in the apartment and if I was a drug user. They thought I had drugged you. Jesus, that is cold, man. They got into some pretty personal shit. I mean they had a psychiatrist there and everything. I don't even remember having my finger in your glass that night. I was pretty hammered too, ya know. As for the laptop, well this part you might actually be annoyed at me about. I was feeling bad for you having to deal with all that shit. So, when I got to your apartment I decided to take your laptop with me. That was your laptop I was on when you interrupted me. I was actually in the middle of deleting and blocking all the nasty stuff on there that was making the situation worse. I knew you would flip out, so that's why I slammed it down when you surprised me. Of course the cops didn't see it that way when they searched my apartment and found it hidden under my bed. They were sure I was the guy." He looks hurt as he speaks and I feel embarrassed.

"Jesus, thanks for making me feel even worse about the situation." I say it in a jokey manner, but he knows I am serious. He takes a moment to have an ironic laugh about the whole situation.

"Yeah, it was pretty hard to explain my way out of that one without looking guilty. I found your phone while I was getting the keys to your apartment out of your bag. I was trying to get into it to do the same as your laptop, but couldn't get past your access code. That's why I pretended I didn't know where it was."

I interrupt him again, "Listen, Zane, you don't have to justify your actions to me."

"No, it's okay. I want to. So, when you wanted to go get your charger, I reacted like that because I had seen all the shit on your laptop. Not just all the creepy emails and texts from Sammy's phone but all the hate mail and shit talkers. I was trying to keep you away from it, but I know now it wasn't the right way of going about it. When Roberts showed up, I had no idea why you were acting so strange. Little did I know that you thought he was saving you from a psychopath." We both chuckle again at the absurdity.

"What were you planning on hurting me with then?"

I look at him embarrassed, "Anything I could get my hands on. I was eyeing up the pots and pans, but the kitchen knives were the weapon of choice."

"Well then, I'm just glad it didn't get that far, and you thought *I* was the psychopath?" We both chuckle as his observation makes a solid argument.

"Then there was the phone call into the show. I mean for one, it didn't sound anything like me, and, two, I was with the guys and it was just after showing my hairy ass on national television."

"Oh shit, I knew it was you." I momentarily forget the gravity of the situation and roar laughing at confirmation of the ass belonging to Zane. Luckily he joins me.

"I'm sorry, I know this is serious, but I just got the mental image of it in my head again. I knew it was you."

"Yeah, my secret is out. I drew the short straw, damn those guys. So anyway, the cops pushed me on that for hours and I kept telling them to just go ask the guys; I never left their sight until the show finished. I wasn't going to miss a minute of you on there. Even though I had an explanation for everything, I actually started to sound so guilty. I could see them neatly fitting the pieces together. I don't know how long I was in there for, but I know I would have just signed a full confession to get the barrage of inane questions to end. Eventually they casually informed me that I was free to go. No explanation was given."

I put my head into my hands, "I know I keep saying it. I don't know how else to say it, I'm just so sorry that I put you through all of that. I know the press were outside and somehow knew about you being taken into custody. I'm sure they made your life hell."

He gives me a knowing look, "Yeah, but it's nothing I couldn't handle." I knew he was keeping just how bad he got slammed in the papers from me.

"I am actually glad I got to hear your side of things and that I got to tell you my side. Now that I have heard what was going on in your mind, I understand a bit better. I can see why things started to point towards me. I just wasn't sure where it had all come from and that is what has been driving me crazy. Thank you for telling me." I can't believe how understanding he is being,

"I'm so glad we are having this talk. Thank you for being so understanding. I don't think I would be in your position." He reaches out his hand and places it in mine. His gesture makes me smile. The sun has almost disappeared and the night is edging its way closer. A cool breeze replaces the warmth. Zane removes his jacket and wraps it around my shoulders like the true gentleman that he is.

"Now, you don't have to or anything, but do you want to tell me what actually happened that day? I know it's traumatic, so I will completely understand if you don't want to." In my preparation I hadn't planned on actually getting this far. It's something I had spent weeks trying to forget about,
trying to force those images out of my head, but I knew he deserved to know. He holds my hand tight to let me know he is there for me.

"I can try. It all happened so fast that some of it is blurry in my mind. So, when I got back to my apartment from the station, I plugged my cell in. There were dozens of texts from Sammy's number. I started reading through some of them. They were just quotes from famous artists and stuff, but then I noticed the timeline. They had all been sent ten minutes from each other that day. The texts spanned the time that you were in custody, right up to the moment I was reading them. I quickly realized it couldn't be you sending them, so I tried to call Roberts. Just as I pressed call, I heard a noise from the kitchen. I went to see what it was and then someone grabbed me from behind and knocked me out with chloroform." Zane mouths 'what' but doesn't make any sound.

"Next thing I knew, I woke up in a loft, tied to a chair by my arms and legs. That's when I saw him for the first time. Well, I thought it was the first time. Turns out he was the guy that bought my three paintings from Lady Miriam that time. So, he had been obsessed with me for all those years. He was disgusting, fat and smelly." I close my eyes and his image is there, standing over me with a scalpel in his hand. I try to shake it off and continue.

"He tried to explain himself to me. He actually believed he was protecting me. He kept talking about how 'they' were going to get me, but he wouldn't explain who 'they' were. There were demented paintings that he had done all over the room. Then he showed me the paintings of mine he had bought at the auction. The sick bastard was convinced I had microchips implanted under my skin, so he knocked me out and tried to cut them out."

Zane can't help but wince, "Jesus, Megan." I slowly roll up my left sleeve to show him the mutilated scars he has left me with. My once perfect tattoos now an incomprehensible mess. He looks at me with pity in his eyes. For once it's pity I reciprocate.

"Of course he didn't find any. He did my other arm and my neck too, but told me he was going to try again later. I was covered in blood and he started stitching up the skin. All the time he was talking about protecting me; he tried to justify the stalking as keeping me safe. He admitted killing Spike that night. He thought he was working for 'them', the sick bastard. I don't know if the cops or anyone told you, but he also murdered Sammy too." I can tell by the utter shock etched on Zane's face that this was new information to him. I couldn't bring myself to tell the other guys at the shop yet.

"What? But why? How?"

"I'm sorry, I thought you knew. He cut Sammy's brakes, that's why he crashed that night. He thought he was one of them. Now I have

Ink Princess

the blood of two deaths on my hands. I know I have to live the rest of my life with the knowledge that it is my fault they are both dead."

Zane is still stunned by my revelation. I really would have worded it better if I had realized he didn't know. I just presumed the cops would have told the guys by now.

"It's not your fault, Megan. That sick freak killed them. There's nothing you could have done. You didn't know what he was capable of."

"I know, but I just think maybe if I hadn't of met you guys or just moved away when he started all this shit, then none of this would have happened. I've carried bad karma around all my life. Maybe I just shouldn't be alive." (A simple flap of a butterfly's wings can change the course of the future, for better or for worse.)

Zane reaches over and pulls me into a hug. "Don't fucking say that; you have to know that none of this is your fault." I let a few tears out in the embrace of the hug. When we resume our positions, Zane's eyes say, 'And what happened next?' But he doesn't want to push me.

"So anyway, he had untied my hands while he was doing the cutting. I had asked him for a glass of water and then held the glass in my hands. I was planning on smashing him over the head with it. He said he was taking me to his house. As soon as his back was turned, I was set to pounce, but then he ruined my plan when he told me he had to knock me out to move me. Just as he was coming at me with a rag full of chloroform, I was getting ready to smash the glass up into his face. That's when the SWAT team burst in. They threw flash grenades; the noise was unbelievable. There was about fifteen heavily armed cops and Detective Roberts. My phone call had reached him and he knew something was up when I didn't answer his calls back. He rushed over to my apartment block and checked the security footage on the cameras. He managed to get a plate number for the white transit van he used to transport me and traced it back to the warehouse. He traced the vehicle back to him and pulled his file. I can never thank him enough. He saved my life that day; he's a truly great man."

"I was so disorientated from the blast I didn't notice he had picked up one of the scalpels he used to cut me open and was now behind me holding it to my neck. Roberts tried to reason with him, saying he knew about 'them' and wanted him to help track them down. His reasoning didn't work and he raised the scalpel to ram it into my neck. That's when one of the snipers shot him." I do feel like I am reciting the scene of a blockbuster movie as I talk. This stuff doesn't happen to normal people. If I hadn't been there, I wouldn't believe it myself.

***

George Patterson, aged forty-two, didn't die that day. He was shot in the shoulder; the bullet just missed the subclavian artery. After being treated at the hospital, he was then committed to Brymore Mental Institution in New York where he awaits trial. Roberts assures me that he will never see the light of day. He described him as being 'one tin foil hat away from complete insanity'. As it transpired, this was not an isolated incident. He had a record that stretched back as far as the early eighties. Convictions for assault, theft, arson, harassment, fraud and kidnapping.

He had served some time in prison, but had long since fallen off the radar of the cops. He worked as an IT specialist in the security sector. Pretty ironic really. This is where he honed his skills in technology and was able to go undetected for so long. His daughter that he spoke of had been killed in a hit and run by a drunk driver. She was only ten when she died. This spiraled his already mentally unstable mind into a paranoid psychotic one. His belief that 'they' took her became a reality in his mind. His wife has been missing since 1995. His conspiracy theories consisted of his belief that the American Government were taking citizens and running experiments on them. He believed they were building an army of superhumans to take control of the world. Anybody who got in their way were killed. For some reason he chose me as the replacement for his deceased daughter and he swore to protect me from the numerous secret agents trying to 'get me'. They raided his home and found hundreds of pictures he had taken of me along with detailed plans of my kidnapping. Roberts did not go into detail, but they had found a hidden bunker under his house. Surely this was the tomb that awaited me if he had taken me there.

  I truly wish he had died that day. I hate the feeling of knowing he is still out there. It doesn't matter that he is locked up, I can still feel his soul living and breathing. I don't want his thoughts to be ones of me. I picture him there with his disgusting nails, still deep in his delusions that what he did was the right thing. I hate that he may never know remorse for what he did. I regret not being brave enough to tell him how twisted his sick mind was. I am not one to pray, but I pray every night that I hear of his death. I walk around knowing that if he ever does get out of there, he is coming to finish the job that he started.

***

Zane and I walk back along the pier in complete silence. There are no more words left to say at this point; his arm tightly wrapped around my shoulder as we walk says it all. When we reach the end, the silence is broken, "So, I think it's time we went for a drink. Do you know any good bars around here?" I smile. It feels like I have my best friend back.

"Yeah, I know a place. I'm not sure they will let your kind in though, a bit classier up this side of the country."

Zane slaps me playfully on the shoulder, "Oh, you sassy little bitch." We both laugh and continue our leisurely stroll towards the bar. ZEDS is a rock bar nestled amongst the fish mongers and hardware stores. As we reach it, Zane takes one look at the neon lighting and crude electric blue painted walls and says, "Oh yeah, classy as hell." This time I playfully punch him. We push open the guitar shaped doors and the noise of AC/DC hits our eardrums like a hammer meeting an anvil. We make our way through the crowds of people, some of which are head banging to the beat of the music. We laugh as we try to avoid the mounds of hair swaying in the air. Hot, sweaty and noisy, just the way I like it. As we turn the corner in search of a seat, the sight in front of me stops me dead in my tracks. Emotions hit me from every angle. I cannot believe what I am seeing. Over the deafening noise I can hear my name.

Zane has stopped and turned to look at me. He wears a cunning smile on his face. Is this his doing? It has to be! Right in front of me is my family. They are all here, Lou, Frankie, Mike, Trent and Billy. I wear the stupidest grin as the guys wave me over. I shout into Zane's ear as we walk, "How the hell did you know we'd come here?"

He smiles knowingly, "C'mon, Megan, we are your brothers. We know you better than anyone, and, besides, we know you are anything but classy." We both burst into laughter. Laughter that continues long into the night. I may not know where the next path is going to take me, but for right now I am home. Here with my family again, amongst the people who truly care for me in this crazy world.

Maybe, just maybe, I do belong on this planet after all.

Baz Black

Baz Black is a Piercer and Body Modification artist from Ireland. He owns a Tattoo and Piercing studio in Co.Louth and has pierced professionally for over twelve years. He is also an internationally published model, a working actor, and drummer for the band 'Amongst the Wolves'

You can find him here-

www.bazblackpiercing.com

facebook.com/bazblackpiercer

facebook.com/bazblackpiercing

Email- bazblackpiercing@hotmail.com

Made in the USA
Charleston, SC
21 June 2016